She heard a moan, low and soft.

Realized it had risen from her. Felt vaguely like she should pull away, but nowhere could she find the strength—or the desire—to do it. The only desire she had was to stay right here, to savor his arms around her and to glory in this mouth on hers. She just might be going crazy, turning into that erratic woman her ex had accused her of being. Some still-functioning part of her mind was sounding a warning, but the heat building in her was unlike anything she'd ever felt. Once she would have said nothing on earth could ever make her throw caution to the winds again.

Apparently, Cooper Grant could.

★ ★ ★

"Like" us on Facebook at
www.facebook.com/RomanticSuspenseBooks
and check us out on www.Harlequin.com!

Dear Reader,

I live in a world that practically revolves around boats. You can't be near Puget Sound for long without it soaking into your bones. I was always a sailboat hound. I learned at a local Sea Scout base, in a thing called a Sabot. Boxy and maybe eight feet long, it had room for you and maybe a dog, if he wasn't too excitable. It was perfect for a relaxing afternoon, you just ignored the seat and plopped crossways, your backside center bottom, feet hanging over one gunnel, head resting on the other, one hand on the rudder, the other full of lunch. As long as the wind stayed lazy, you were golden. But my husband, being a motor guy, was all about powerboats, the faster the better.

Now, as I watch boats travel the Sound, I wonder about the stories they carry. The huge ones, the container ships, fishing boats and the cruise liners, are obvious. But it's the small, private ones that wake up my muse. Where are those people headed? Just to enjoy a day on the water? Perhaps to show visiting guests or family the area? Or perhaps to avoid those visiting guests or family for a while?

Or perhaps, there's a whole different story....

Justine Davis

JUSTINE DAVIS

Enemy Waters

ROMANTIC
SUSPENSE

Recycling programs
for this product may
not exist in your area.

ISBN-13: 978-0-373-27729-2

ENEMY WATERS

Printed in U.S.A.

JUSTINE DAVIS

lives on Puget Sound in Washington. Her interests outside of writing are sailing, doing needlework, horseback riding and driving her restored 1967 Corvette roadster—top down, of course.

Justine says that, years ago, during her career in law enforcement, a young man she worked with encouraged her to try for a promotion to a position that was at the time occupied only by men. "I succeeded, became wrapped up in my new job, and that man moved away, never, I thought, to be heard from again. Ten years later, he appeared out of the woods of Washington State, saying he'd never forgotten me and would I please marry him. With that history, how could I write anything but romance?"

For my sweet, beloved, wonderful girl,
the most perfect dog in all of the world.
When my time comes, when the last golden days
wind down, may I face it with one tenth the grace
and spirit you have. I know by the time this sees light,
you will likely have gone, and it breaks my heart.

But never having had you would have been worse. We
thought we were rescuing you, but indeed, it was you
who saved us. Me especially, after the worst happened.

He'll be waiting for you when you get there,
sweet girl, that man you loved so much
and took care of so well.

I love you, my beautiful, clever,
whimsical Decoy Dawg. And as someone once said,
if dogs don't go to heaven, I want to go where they go.
I'll see you there, sunshine.

Chapter 1

She didn't know he was watching her.

Cooper Grant sipped at his coffee leisurely, as if he had all the time in the world. Which he did, as long as she was here. And since the little café had just opened for the day, and her shift had obviously just begun, she was going to be here for a while.

The woman flicked a glance in his direction, but again it wasn't as if she thought he was watching her. She didn't seem aware of him in particular; she was keeping her eye on all the occupied tables. Which were numerous this time of day; the Waterfront was obviously the place to meet in the morning in tiny Port Murphy.

Of course, he thought wryly, it was also the only place in town open at this hour, and darned near the only place in town at all.

No, he didn't think she knew he was watching her.

But she acted like she was afraid someone was. Odd.

He took another long sip, savored the rich flavor; the little town's only full-time eatery had the coffee down right. And the food, too, if his nose was any judge; the smells wafting around were enough to make him wish he'd ordered a real breakfast instead of just toast and coffee. The place might be old and look a bit shabby, but the kitchen in the back corner was spotless, and the thin, wiry man with the poker face and the Navy tattoo on his forearm ran it with what Cooper guessed was military precision.

In the moments when she was busy taking an order from a group of four who were seated at a corner table, he took another glance out the window. It was hard not to get lost in the postcard-worthy tableau. The picturesque little cove dotted with boats—one of them his own, on an offshore mooring—the rows of little houses, some brightly colored enough to stand out like gems scattered on the hillsides, and the already snow-capped mountains in the distance.

Getting downright poetic, Grant, he thought. And turned his attention back to his quarry, the brunette with the pixie haircut, the heavy, dark-rimmed glasses, and the oversized T-shirt with the café logo. This was about the only time she was still, when taking an order. The rest of the time she flitted around like a hummingbird, always moving, never lingering, but keeping everything efficiently handled.

As she turned to take the next order his gaze shot back to the right side of her face, and the small mole just in front of her ear. His mouth quirked. He didn't really blame himself for needing the reassurance; she'd transformed herself so completely that if it wasn't for that mole, he'd still be searching.

But once he'd seen it, he'd compared the other things that didn't change, the shape of that ear, the lines of the jaw, nose, mouth—and once he'd gotten close enough to see that despite the black-rimmed glasses she was wearing contact lenses, which would explain the brown eyes instead of blue—he'd known he'd found her.

He took a sip of the excellent coffee, thinking about the phone call he was looking forward to making, to tell his client his wait was over. He pictured the reunion between Tristan Jones and his little sister, and felt the warmth of a satisfaction that was all too rare in his life.

Although he did wonder about the transformation. A haircut

was one thing, but the dye job, and above all the disguising contact lenses? What was that all about? He understood the need for change after tragedy and trauma—understood it all too well—but what did totally changing your appearance accomplish?

It had to be a girl thing, he decided finally. And he'd given up trying to understand those.

He watched as she turned in the order from the table in the corner, spoke briefly with the cook, checked to be sure no new diners had arrived, then picked up the pot of fresh coffee off the warmer. He actually enjoyed watching her. He appreciated efficiency, in whatever realm. She certainly didn't act like a nut case, but what did he know?

She started, as usual, with the table nearest the door. If she ran true to form, she would circle back to the counter after the tables, starting at the far end, which meant she would get to him last. Which was why, after three days of observing her, he'd chosen this seat near the door.

Well, that and the fear that if she realized he was looking for her she might panic and run. He wasn't sure why she was so edgy, but he couldn't deny that she clearly was. No ordinary person on an ordinary day was so hyperaware of everything around her; the slightest movement outside, even a seagull landing on the railing, drew her eye. He wondered if she was having some kind of trouble that was making her so wary, but it seemed at odds with this place that appeared to be the epitome of peace and quiet.

He watched as she refilled cup after cup. She was quick yet didn't seem hurried, a nice knack in this job.

You'd never guess that eight months ago she was seen more often in silk, satin and stiletto heels than jeans and baggy T-shirts, Cooper thought.

And then she was there, pot in hand, giving him the practiced smile of a waitress as she gestured with the coffeepot.

"Top it off for you?"

He nodded, pushing the heavy mug toward her on the polished countertop. "Great coffee."

"It keeps people coming," she said with that same, neutral smile.

"I can see why. Not," he said as he took the mug back, "that there's much competition."

To her credit, the smile widened into something more genuine, less practiced. "There is that," she agreed.

In that moment an odd sensation swept through him. He felt the strongest urge to violate his client's orders and tell her. To put an end to the hell she'd been through, was still living in. Maybe it was simply that that had made her so twitchy; things like that awful night affected different people in different ways. He was living proof of that.

But Tristan Jones was calling the shots, and he kept silent. About that, anyway. Instead he went with a safe newcomer-to-local question that had the added advantage of being true.

"Cooper Grant," he said, holding out a hand. She gestured with the coffeepot, dodging the handshake. He let it pass; he was still feeling his way, carefully. "I'm looking for a place to dock my boat for a while. You're a local, right? Any ideas?"

She set down the pot. Her brow furrowed very slightly as she pondered the inquiry. In an unconscious gesture she reached up beneath the glasses and pushed at the skin around her right eye. Then she caught herself and stopped.

Contacts are bothering her, he thought. And wondered again why she'd done it. If it hadn't been for the glasses, he would have thought she just wanted a change, some women were that way, he guessed. But both? That spoke of disguise, and that stumped him.

"There's a couple of guest berths at the marina," she said in answer to his question.

"Checked. They're full."

She nodded as if she'd expected as much. "How long?"

"Forty-three."

To most people, that sounded fairly big. To someone used

to the kind of yachts owned by the people Tanya and Jeremy Brown mingled with, it was a runabout. But her only reaction was to get more thoughtful.

"Power? Sail?"

This might actually work, he thought. He'd learned from the woman behind the register that she was renting a place by the water, so he'd risked it on the chance she knew somebody with a dock. And the way she was reacting made him think he was right. She had thought of something. Something that perhaps depended on the depth of his boat's keel. Thankfully, his answer should resolve that.

"Power."

"Where is it now?"

"On the last mooring out in the cove. Not sure I trust it, either. Seems a bit loose. Last night I swear I drifted a few feet."

"You're sleeping out there?"

"For the most part I live aboard, go wherever I want."

He watched her face for a reaction; living aboard a boat tended to be something people saw the appeal of either immediately, or never. She appeared to fall into the first group, judging by the slight smile that curved her mouth. The mouth that was still cupid's-bow perfect, even without the high sheen of fancy lipsticks or gloss that had been the norm in the pictures her brother had sent him.

"Sounds nice," she said.

"No roots," he pointed out, since that was the complaint most women had. Then wondered why he'd bothered.

"No ties," she answered, as if it were a good thing.

Interesting, he thought. Most women thought that a negative. "Well, one," he amended. "Every couple of months I go check on my mom."

He couldn't believe he'd pulled that one out. True, it usually won him some points with whatever woman he was trying to impress, and it had the advantage of being fact. But this woman was just a job; he wasn't trying to impress her. The woman in the photographs, maybe, but this quiet, plain little wren?

God, I really am that shallow, he thought ruefully.

And he'd lost track of one of his most basic rules; outward appearances rarely told the full story.

"Where's your mom?"

"Over on the dry side," he said. "Spokane."

"Hard to sail there from here."

"That's what buses are for."

Something flickered in her expression, and he wondered if she was thinking of her own bus trip here. But whatever it was, she didn't dwell on it.

"How long do you need the berth for?"

"Week, maybe two. I've got some maintenance and tuning to do. She's overdue."

With luck, he'd be done here well before two weeks, probably closer to two days once he made that call, but he was toying with the idea of staying anyway. There was something immensely appealing—and soothing—about the little town and its peaceful, charming waterfront.

"You know a place?" he prompted, when she didn't go on.

"Maybe. The guy's pretty picky about who he lets hang around. He'd want to know about you first."

"Me? I'm harmless."

"He's not going to take your word for it."

"Then whose word will he take?"

"Mine," she said.

Cooper leaned back. The bar stool at the counter put him nearly at eye level with her if he sat up straight, as his mother had always nagged him about. He lifted an elbow to rest it on the slatted back of the old-fashioned stool.

"So he trusts you," he said.

"Yes."

Interesting, he thought. Who had she gotten to trust her that much in the less than six months she'd been here? He knew it was only that. He'd started in Seattle, had been afraid she'd vanished into the masses of the metro area, or become one of the half million or so in the city proper. But then a routine check of the city's bus terminal, something he practically yawned through, had turned up a rather grandfatherly ticket seller who remembered her. She'd cut her hair by then, but she hadn't yet dyed it or added the brown contacts, or she probably would have gone unnoticed and unrecognized.

She'd bought a ticket to Port Angeles, but he hadn't found any trace of her there. That had started him checking all the bus stops before that, with the nagging awareness that Port Angeles was the starting point for ferry service to Canada, which would open a whole new can of worms.

Working on the assumption she wouldn't have left the country, he'd spent a long three weeks checking small towns in the area. He'd hit the edge of his patience for the drudge work in the middle of that third week; only the knowledge that Jones was paying the freight—and in turn most of the bills that had made him take the job in the first place—kept him moving. Then three days ago he'd walked into the Waterfront Café and taken a second look, then a third, at the unassuming woman who had refilled his coffee mug.

"Guess I'll just have to get you to trust me, then," he said, giving her his best smile, one he'd once been told could charm hornets.

She seemed immune. In fact, her gaze narrowed with suspicion. His own brow furrowed slightly; she didn't act like a woman in emotional turmoil. Oddly, the main sense he was getting from her wasn't even the grief he would have expected, although it was there, visible even in the masked eyes. The main thing he was feeling from her was…fear.

That made no sense. Unless she really had gotten into some kind of trouble since she'd disappeared off the radar down south. That was a possibility he hadn't considered until now. Had she picked up some kind of stalker or something, was that the reason behind the edginess, the constant awareness of her surroundings?

"Are you all right?" he asked, dropping the effort to charm.

She seemed startled by the abrupt switch. "I'm fine." She picked up the coffeepot and started to turn away.

"Nell," he said, using the name on the small plastic badge she wore on the Waterfront T-shirt. She turned back. Still looked wary. He hesitated. He'd found her, that had been his job, it didn't really matter if she liked him or not. At least, not as far as the job was concerned. The instructions had been crystal; if he found her he was to say nothing until her brother could get here. Simple.

At least, it should be.

"I wasn't trying to snow you," he said. "It's just— I've been looking for three weeks, and…I'm tired."

It was all true, if not all of the truth. And that, he thought, took it out of the realm of totally cold calculation. Well, almost; he had to admit he was counting on the fact that she looked tired enough herself to be able to relate.

She wavered, but the suspicion lingered. "I didn't think temporary berths were that hard to find up here."

Up here. A true local likely wouldn't have added that. But somebody from down south—especially as far as L.A.—might. He hadn't had much doubt left, but that helped erase it.

"It's the combination," he said.

"Combination?"

"A temporary berth and a marine supply store that will have what I need."

And that, again, was the truth.

"And a place closer to home to park a motorcycle?"

So she'd noticed that. It didn't surprise him, after watching her watch…everything.

"Exactly," he said.

"You carry it on the boat?"

He nodded. "Built ramps to offload it at a dock, but getting it in and out of the dinghy's a bit much. Rowing it? No way."

One corner of her mouth quirked, as if at the image. She turned, set the nearly empty coffeepot back on the warming plate, busied herself with starting a fresh pot. He could almost feel her thinking, trying to decide. He wondered who the guy with the dock was, why she seemed…almost protective of him. Boyfriend?

That opened a whole new box of questions, so he left it alone for now. And tried to ignore the little jab the idea gave him. What did it matter to him if she'd found somebody in this remote paradise?

She turned back suddenly, decisively. "I'll talk to my friend. Maybe he'll at least talk to you about it."

"Thank you," he said, meaning it. And wondering why she sounded unhappy about it.

He left the café feeling satisfied. He'd found his quarry and she was alive and well, if very different in appearance. That satisfied him even more, that she hadn't fooled him. He would make that phone call to her brother, who would be delighted and not quibble about the final bill he was going to get, which meant Cooper could pay off all his bills and have enough left over to be picky about his next job.

Although this one had been a lot better than the typical domestic situation; spying on a cheating spouse, a thieving son or a daughter into dangerous drugs was not very uplifting. Tracking down a woman who'd vanished in a paroxysm of grief and telling her the person she was grieving for hadn't really died was something else again. He had to admit the story had gotten to him. He could get to liking this kind of case.

Again he wished he could just tell her now. But her brother had insisted—it had been so bad, he said, that she'd never believe it if she didn't see him in the flesh, alive and walking around, albeit scarred. Besides, he wanted to see her face when she saw him. His right, Cooper thought. He was the brother, and he was paying the freight.

He just didn't like the idea of her going another moment thinking her own husband had shot and killed her brother.

Chapter 2

She took off the plastic badge with "Nell" on it, tossing it down on the table next to her keys. Her name choices had been limited to those attached to the fake Social Security numbers available from the underground dealer she'd bought the ID from. She'd had to have it to work, and this name at least she felt a personal connection with, so she'd taken it. She'd felt a qualm when she'd realized that in fact it probably belonged either to someone who had died, or some child not old enough to work yet, but since she'd never take the money out she figured it would be all right.

"Nell!"

It was Roger Donlan's voice, calling out in his usual cheery way. Her landlord normally was in a good mood, although she suspected sometimes it was a cover for sadness, a feeling she understood all too well. His wife of forty years had died nearly ten years ago, and the man still missed her. She wondered what it must be like to have loved a spouse so much that nearly a decade later the pain was still so strong.

She would feel that way about her brother, she knew. She would never get over losing Tris. She could only hope to deal with it as well as Roger Donlan had, building a life around the hole, a busy and full life.

But Roger didn't have the cloud hanging over him that she did, Nell told herself. She thought of herself as Nell Parker now. She'd felt well rid of the hated last name, along with the rest of her life when she'd taken off into a night howling with fifty-mile-per-hour Santa Ana winds. She liked Nell a lot better than she'd liked Tanya Jones Brown, and what she'd become.

A shiver went through her as the memories rose up. It seemed as surreal now as it had then, and just as impossible. She remembered the moment when she'd stopped her car at a light, in total disbelief that she was sitting there shivering in clothes soaked with Tris's blood.

She still couldn't believe it. Tristan had been her rock, her bulwark, her hero, since the day she'd been born. He'd played with her when most big brothers would have shrugged her off in disgust, he'd watched out for her when she'd begun to explore the world and he'd been her protector always. From bullies to boys with wicked intent, Tris had always been there for her.

And she would mourn him, grieve for him, forever, just as Roger grieved his lost love.

"Nell? You there?" The words were accompanied by a polite tap on her door.

"Here," she called out, and went to open the door.

Roger was seventy-two years old, but he looked at least a decade younger, maybe more. He was active, strong and Tanya wished she had half his energy. The man worked from dawn to dark, and his property here showed it. He dabbled in topiary, as evidenced by the pair of leafy, rearing horses that guarded his driveway, he had a garden and orchard the envy of the whole town and he was cook enough to make good use of his yield.

He'd also converted her place, once a small, four-stall barn, into a comfortable granny flat, doing the work himself. Quality work; it was solid, well thought out, and she was lucky it had been available at a rent she could afford. She suspected he was giving her a break on the price, but she hadn't been in a position to argue about it.

"Fresh stuffed artichokes tonight," he said. "And the last of the Copper River salmon from the freezer. Join me?"

"Love to. I'll bring the wine."

It was the only repayment he would allow her. They'd fallen into a habit of sharing a meal at least once a week, and she'd taken to stocking a couple of bottles of wine for those occasions, after learning he loved to experiment with different kinds and was anything but a wine snob.

"Always looking for that unexpected little treasure," he said.

Yes, she would do well to model herself on her gruff, kind-hearted landlord.

It was after the luscious meal, when they were savoring the last of the surprisingly good—and cheap—bottle of Pinot Grigio she'd brought, that she steeled herself to mention the man in the café. She was hesitant, somewhat selfishly. She'd found a sort of…not peace, that had eluded her, but a sort of calm here. A place to search for that peace. And she didn't want it disrupted. On the other hand, Roger was giving her such a deal on the rent, she couldn't help wondering if his finances could use the boost of even a couple of weeks of renting out his dock.

She had no right to withhold the opportunity, she told herself, and brought it up.

"A guy in the café today was asking about renting a berth, to do some work on his boat. The marina's full, even the guest slips."

"Usually is, this time of year," Roger said, looking at her over the rim of his glass. "You thinking of mine?"

"Just mentioning it." She had the feeling Roger would do it as a favor to her, if he thought it was a friend of hers, so she hastened to clarify. "He's just a guy who's been coming in for two or three days. Not somebody I know."

"You like him?"

"I don't know him," she repeated. "He seems nice enough, now that I've talked to him a little. When he first came in he… spooked me."

Roger set down his wineglass, frowning. "Spooked you?"

She shrugged; she hadn't really meant to say that. She knew it was just her own wariness that made her feel every stranger was watching her. It was one of the reasons she'd ended up here in Port Murphy; the small size of the town made strangers easier to spot.

"He's probably all right. I'm just cautious."

"I know." The old man's expression softened.

"I'll tell him whatever you want," she said. "Like I said, I just thought I'd mention it. It would only be for a week or two, he said."

Roger studied her, and she almost held her breath, hoping he'd let the subject of trust drop. After a moment, he did. "What kind of boat?"

"Power. Forty-three feet, he said."

"That would fit."

She nodded. "You said yours was forty-five, so I figured."

"Depends. The turn's a little tight. But if he's any good at maneuvering, it should be fine."

"Don't know. I didn't get into details with him. Didn't want him getting his hopes up, or ending up putting pressure on you, so I didn't even tell him who you were."

Roger lifted a brow at her. "Would he bother you, being around?"

"I could avoid him for two weeks." She ran a finger around the stem of her glass. "I don't know what he'd be able to pay. He's a live-aboard, but apparently by choice."

"Rootless or feckless?"

"I don't know." She gave him the best smile she could manage. "Could go either way."

"When's he there?"

"Mornings, usually. Right after we open."

Roger nodded. "I'll come in. Feel him out. Get a gauge on him before I commit to anything."

She nodded. "Just talk to him and see what you think."

"I'll do that. I'm a pretty good judge of people."

Not quite as good as you think, or I wouldn't be here, she thought.

Later, she stood on the dock in question and watched the sunset over the Olympic Mountains. Tris would like it here, she thought. But he would have lasted about a week and then been ready to head back to the city. Any city. He had appreciated nature, but Tristan Jones was a city boy through and through; he fed on the chaos, thrived on the pulsing energy. It was his natural habitat as much as this was for the bald eagle she spotted gliding toward the trees in the fading light, and he always went back.

Or had, she amended, painfully correcting herself yet again. You'd think she'd be used to it by now, after all these months. But she wasn't. How did you think about a person as alive and vital as Tris in the past tense?

She sank down onto the dock, huddling into herself as the pain swept her anew. It wasn't cold, yet she shivered as she sat there, arms wrapped around herself, a poor substitute for the arms she'd never feel again. Her big brother, laughing at her, teasing her endlessly, yet ever and always there for her when she needed him.

She sat there for a long time, putting off going to bed. Because sleep was no longer welcome in her life. Sleep meant dreams. Bad ones. During the day she could at least fight to keep them at bay; at night, they had free rein and she was helpless against them.

But eventually she would make herself go. She was nearing exhaustion, she could feel it. Two or three hours of sleep a night—if she was lucky—wasn't cutting it.

Besides, she thought as she finally got to her feet and walked back toward the little garden house, nightmares were the least of what she deserved.

The little building was painted yellow and white, bright, clean and cheerful against the sometimes gray weeks on end of the northwest. It looked charming and welcoming, and in fact she felt more at home here than she ever had in that big, cold McMansion behind wrought, or, as she'd always thought of them, overwrought iron gates.

But there was no ease of welcome for her here, or anywhere. She didn't deserve that, either. She had done this, to herself and to Tris. Her beloved big brother had died in her arms, and it was her stupid emotions and poor judgment that had killed him.

She might as well have pulled the trigger herself.

Chapter 3

"You're certain?"

"Absolutely."

Between yawns—the phone had rung a few minutes after 5:00 a.m.—Cooper explained it all to Jones: the hair, the contact lenses and why he was sure anyway. Then to confirm, he sent the photo he'd surreptitiously snapped with his smartphone, a profile shot showing the mole just in front of her right ear.

"Yes," Tristan finally agreed, "it looks like her, despite the changes. The mole is in the right place, and her chin, and nose, those are right. How long has she been there?"

"Just over six months. Arrived on the same day we know she got off a bus in Seattle, via a bus from Portland. It's her, no matter what she's calling herself now."

"What *is* she calling herself now?"

"Nell Parker."

Cooper heard Tristan Jones's breath catch.

"That means something?"

"Nell was our mother's middle name."

Cooper grinned, although the man couldn't see it. "You really believe me now?"

"Yes."

There was a world of satisfaction in the man's voice, and Cooper thought this was going to be a hell of a reunion. But he was curious about something, so he asked.

"So, why the disguise? Why would she do that?"

"Tanya was always doing that," he said. "Even as a kid, she played at being different people. One time she dyed her hair pink and blue. Freaked the family out, but I think she thought it made her more interesting. She liked the attention."

The mousy, subdued persona didn't seem like someone looking for attention, but Tanya Jones Brown likely wasn't the same woman she'd once been. Nobody went through something like that and came out unchanged.

"She seems...awfully nervous."

"I told you, Tanya is high-strung and high maintenance. She has been ever since our mother died, and I'm sure what's happened has only made that worse. I'm just glad you actually found her. Thank God."

Cooper didn't have the patience for high maintenance, couldn't imagine loving someone like that. Yet women like that seemed to own the men in their lives. And this one had her husband and her brother dancing to her tune, it seemed. At least, the woman in that photo did. He wasn't so sure about the woman he'd been watching for three days.

But he quashed the thought as he talked to the man paying the bills, although in the back of his mind he was figuring that Jones was being kind because he loved his sister, and that Tanya Jones Brown was probably even worse than he said. He just hadn't seen it yet, which puzzled him.

"So, what do you want me to do now?"

"Watch her. Closely. Don't say anything—*anything*—to her about me, don't tell her who you are or why you're there. But don't lose her. I'll be there as soon as I can, but I'm in London."

"London?" Cooper said, startled. But at least it explained the crack-of-dawn call; it was probably lunchtime there.

"Yes. Meetings. It's going to take a few days to extricate myself."

"Wow. Nice job."

Jones had told him his brother-in-law had given him a job after he'd recuperated, but Cooper hadn't known it involved globe-trotting. He wondered if Jeremy Brown had done it out of generosity or guilt, then decided it didn't matter much in the long run. The two men obviously had at least one thing in common; they loved Tanya.

"I'll call you when I'm back stateside and give you a better idea. Just don't lose her!"

"I'll stay on her like those contact lenses," he promised.

After they'd disconnected, Cooper sat on the deck of *The Peacemaker,* looking toward the mountains until the sun began to rise, painting the mountains with the orange and pink of dawn's brush. He watched quietly for a long time, thinking he understood what Tanya/Nell had found here.

And trying to somehow reconcile the portrait her brother painted of a changeable, attention-demanding woman with the quiet, seemingly attention-avoiding woman he'd found here.

Not that it mattered. His job was to keep an eye on her, make sure she didn't vanish again. So, while he would keep to his client's wishes and not say anything to her about why he was here, or about her brother, even that he was still alive, there was no reason he couldn't maintain the contact he'd already made.

Which might, he realized, be easier said than done. So far it had been like stalking that hummingbird he'd thought of: one second there, gone the next. But he had a foot in the door now, and he'd be a fool to give that up.

It took everything she had not to whirl around to look when she heard the sound of a motorcycle engine winding up behind her. It wouldn't be him, she told herself, this bike was coming out from one of the houses on the bluff above the cove.

And even if it was, was she really silly enough to feel a little thrill at the idea? Would she really turn around and stare at the man she'd already been thinking far too much about since the day he'd walked into the café and given her that lazy smile and drawled *thank you* for refilling his cup of coffee?

She kept walking, her eyes determinedly on the sidewalk as she headed for the beginning of the path that ran for the last mile through the waterfront park. She weakened as the whine of the engine neared, giving a quick, almost furtive look to the side, telling herself she was just checking to make sure it wasn't some crazy local kid who might crash or something.

As she reached the start of the park path, the bright red motorcycle shot by her and headed up toward the main road. Indeed a local kid—although she doubted a crazy one—aboard, not even giving her a glance as he rocketed by, crouched over the handlebars as he revved the throttle, apparently content with waking the neighborhood rather than running over unwary pedestrians. He leaned into a sharp right and headed north, probably toward the high school, she thought.

No, it was not the man she'd been thinking far too much about lately. His motorcycle was black and, she thought, a bit smaller. Couldn't keep a huge thing like that red one on a boat, she guessed. Or rather, get it on and off, which would be the point.

And, she thought as she got to where she could see the marina, there his bike was, parked where she'd noticed it before, at the head of the visitor's dock. She supposed he must have tied up at the temporary side tie and offloaded the thing, then gone back to tie up at the offshore mooring.

Her gaze shifted to the end of the dock where the port master's office was. There were only two guest slips in the small marina, and she could see they were still occupied. The season was ending, but it wasn't over yet. Too bad; she'd been half hoping a slip would open up for him.

And half hoping one wouldn't.

You, she told herself with no small amount of chagrin, *are an idiot.*

But no amount of telling herself that, and reminding herself that she'd sworn off entanglements, possibly for good, seemed to make any difference; the lean, rangy man with the crooked smile and the laid-back air had crept into her mind and refused to leave.

He'd probably laugh if he knew, she chided herself silently. She'd successfully turned herself into a quiet, plain, virtually unnoticeable woman, hardly the type a man like that would look at twice, let alone take an interest in. No, this man with the dark hair, strong jaw and light, almost green eyes would require an attractive woman at his side, and any time he spent dabbling with her would be along the lines of a cat playing with a small, insignificant mouse because it amused him.

More like a tiger toying with dinner, she amended grimly.

Or, she thought, a little more charitably, he figured she could do something for him. Like find him that berth for his boat.

On that thought she looked out at the cove. There were about a half-dozen boats tied up to the permanent moorings, cramming in those last, desperate moments of decent weather before the wet fall and winter set in. There were always boats there, Roger had told her; if you didn't take your boat out in the rain up here, you might as well just rent one for two months in the summer and forget it the rest of the year.

The farthest mooring out, he'd said. She looked past two small cabin cruisers, a fishing boat, two sailboats and then out to the last blue-and-white buoy. Secured to it was a boat with a dark blue hull and a white topside. It looked tidy and in good shape from here, although she wasn't sure what she'd expected. Just because he lived aboard didn't mean it had to look like a caricature of a houseboat.

What did you expect, a laundry line strung from bow to stern? He actually moves the thing, so of course it's got to be shipshape to some extent.

She nearly stumbled over an uneven spot in the raked gravel path, realized she was staring at the boat instead of watching where she was going. She yanked her attention back to business, furious with herself. She'd gotten through nearly eight months without focusing on a man outside of the café— except for Roger, but that was completely different—and she'd done just fine. Damned if she was going to let this man shake that, no matter how much he kept snaking into her mind. She wasn't fool enough for that.

She knew she was vulnerable. And she knew even better— far, far too well—that responding to a man, any man, when you were vulnerable carried a very high price. The last time she'd done it, it had ended up destroying her life.

And costing her brother his.

Chapter 4

Guilt, Cooper thought, does crazy things to you. Nobody knew that better than he. He'd lived it for over half his life.

He veered away from that old, well-worn track and kept his mind on the matter at hand. On the woman at hand. The woman he was waiting for, and had been for twenty minutes. Fortunately, the bench he sat on was in a pleasant place, under a sizeable tree and angled to look out over the water to the forested hills on the opposite side of the cove.

He knew she walked to work. He'd overheard someone asking her about it in the café.

"I enjoy it," she'd said, with every evidence of sincerity. "It's only two miles, and I come up the path through the park, along the water. It's beautiful, peaceful—"

"Wet," one of the diners had pointed out.

"Well, yes," she'd said with the most genuine smile he'd seen from her. "But I don't mind that, either. It's the price for all this gorgeous green, isn't it?"

He'd wondered about the sunny attitude at the time. Wondered if she really enjoyed it, or if it was simply that she didn't have a car. She'd left, after all, with virtually nothing. Her brother had told him she'd taken some cash that had been in her husband's desk that night, just under a thousand dollars.

Not much, he'd said, not for Tanya. She was used to living high, he'd said, and he'd been certain she hadn't gotten far on it. But her car had been found near a Greyhound station, and it had been the memory of a favorite family vacation that had made him call an investigator in the northwest.

Cooper was a little surprised that Tristan Jones wasn't canceling everything and hopping on the first available flight, such had been his urgency to find his sister.

But you found her, he told himself, *so no more urgency.*

He felt another jolt of satisfaction, like a warning bell going off in his head. Was he actually starting to enjoy this work? Or was it simply that this time he'd been paid a large chunk up front, that there'd be no chasing down a client reluctant to pay up after he'd gotten what he wanted?

Jones was just a busy guy, Cooper thought. Only busy guys made the kind of money Jones was paying him. In the end, he was going to be buying Cooper all he needed to get *The Peacemaker* shipshape again, and some free time to do it in to boot. He had no complaints. The job had been routine, if a bit tedious, and, more important, lacked the unsavory tinge of so many of the jobs he took simply out of the need to eat.

Just think about how much more you'd have to work if you had the standard issues: rent, car payments, cable TV...wife, kids.

He jumped up and walked down the neatly maintained path—this water's-edge haven was nicely taken care of by the locals—to where he could see a long stretch of it heading down toward the residential neighborhood. Since the other end of the path terminated near the head of the cove and the small commercial district, within a block of the café, he knew she had to come up from there.

He'd ridden it on the bike in reverse, the day after he'd overheard that conversation. At the two miles she'd mentioned, there were three possibilities, three directions she could go after she hit the end of the park path. Down toward the water, and the older houses that had been part of the original town, straight ahead into the houses that went along the main road, or up the hill where the newer neighborhoods were. Problem was, he didn't know exactly what "by the water" had meant, and the café owner hadn't been in the mood to expand on the vague answer.

Hell, around here, *everything* could be seen as "by the water."

He supposed it didn't matter if he didn't know exactly where she lived, as long as he knew where she worked. But he'd feel better if he did. And better yet if he was also in the neighborhood; he hoped whoever it was she'd been thinking of about the dock was close by.

He stood for a moment, looking toward the far end of the path. There was an older couple walking along hand in hand, a kid with a big, shaggy dog and a guy loaded down with fishing gear, all moving at different paces. But no single woman, at least not yet. But it was still early, if she was a fast walker. He returned to his bench. The kid with the dog had paused, texting a message on his cell phone.

Just then a solitary figure came into sight, around the bend in the path about thirty yards away. She was walking steadily but not hastily, slow enough to soak in the ambiance of the water, the trees, the serenity of the setting.

He shoved his hands into the front pockets of his jeans and waited, his head turned toward the natural view of the water, but he kept her solidly in his peripheral vision. He worked on making it seem coincidental; to some women it might be flattering that a man would wait here for the chance to run into them, but this woman was so edgy he wasn't sure what she'd do. It was a good thing he'd been warned, or he'd be wondering what the heck was with her, anyway.

"Right now she's not thinking too clearly," Jones had told him. "She really blames herself, because she called me over to the house that night. To talk about plans for Jeremy's surprise birthday party."

A perfectly normal action that had ended in disaster. In

tragedy. Maybe that was why he'd taken this case in the first place, Cooper thought. Because he knew so damned well how that felt. Go to work one day like any other. And never come home.

He shook off the memory. He'd read the news story Jones had sent. A case of mistaken identity gone mad, resulting in her older brother being shot as a burglar, kidnapper, rapist or whatever her husband had feared. The man had, the article said, taken a lie detector test and passed with flying colors, and the police had closed the case as an accidental shooting.

He had deduced two more things from the article: one, at the time the wounds Jones suffered had been described as fatal. It had been an alert paramedic, Jones told him, who did his job thoroughly and discovered the faint pulse of life still in him. But by then Tanya had vanished.

Jeremy Brown was blameless, Jones had said, he'd thought Tanya in danger and acted accordingly, just as the article said. He'd been devastated, both by what had happened and by Tanya's disappearance. He'd spent months looking for her in Southern California while Jones, as soon as he was able, led the search farther afield. At first that had sounded like an odd division, until he thought about it a little and realized searching the massively populated area would be much tougher, and likely hugely expensive. Jeremy was a well-known fundraiser in a town full of them, James had said, the best of the best. And Tanya had been an asset in that, with her beauty and charm.

Which was the second thing he'd learned from that article: Tanya Jones had been incredibly hot then. Normally it would have been odd that the photo included with the article was not of the shooter or the victim, but the sister of the victim, but one look at it told him why. Any newspaper would jump at the chance to run the glamorous shot of a leggy, beautiful woman with a thick, blond mane of hair, in a floor-length gown that was classy and sexy at the same time.

The woman in the photo was a far cry from the waitress with the short, dark hair and thick-rimmed glasses, dressed in jeans and a baggy shirt that hid any hint of the figure that gown had displayed so well.

The one who was barely fifteen feet away now. Walking slowly, not meandering like someone with all the time in the world to walk in this beautiful place, but like someone lost, aching, looking for a solace even nature's bounty couldn't provide.

Walking wounded, he thought. That was what she looked like. The sight of her churned him up inside, in a way he'd never quite felt before. It kind of echoed the way he'd felt looking at his mother after his father had died, the way he himself had felt. But yet it was different, spiked with instincts he'd never known he had before, to stand between her and anything that might try to hurt her even more.

And it was that confused set of feelings that had put him where he was now.

Just imagine how she feels, he told himself.

Slowly, he began walking toward her.

She spotted him the moment he started to move. She told herself the leap her heart gave was a normal reaction, even here, a thousand safe miles away. Yet that image of a tiger toying with what would eventually become dinner had stuck with her, uncomfortably.

"Hey, Nell!"

His voice was bright, welcoming, the perfect greeting to an acquaintance stumbled upon accidentally. So why didn't she believe it?

"Beautiful morning, isn't it?" he said.

"Yes," she said, unable to summon up anything more than that.

"On your way to work? Will coffee be available?"

"Of course," she answered, aware of the stiffness of her voice.

He dropped the cheer, and she didn't know if that proved

it had been false, or if he was just a nice guy reacting to her own shortness.

"Are you all right? You look like you expect an orca to come charging up out of the cove and attack."

"I was thinking more of tigers," she muttered, not looking at him.

"Tigers?"

He sounded confused, and she risked a glance at him. No, he hadn't changed: same dark, tousled hair, same laid-back, casual manner. Nothing tigerlike about him at all, except the way he moved.

And those eyes, more green than hazel, and with a slightly predatory look. Tiger, indeed.

"You're safe…Nell," he said, with an odd hesitation that made her wonder if he'd forgotten her name in the space of thirty seconds.

Or as if he'd almost called her something else. Fear spiked through her.

"Safety," she said, "is an illusion."

An illusion she doubted she'd ever have again.

Chapter 5

"Cooper Grant, Roger Donlan," she said, pouring them each a cup of coffee. "Have at it, gentlemen."

Introductions made, Nell walked away and went about her business. It was a busy morning at the Waterfront, a gorgeously sunny fall weekend morning had brought people out in droves.

They were at a table for two in one corner, the quietest corner, behind a little stub wall that seemed to separate it from the rest of the dining room. Interesting that she'd seated them here, Cooper thought. Good place for a business meeting like this.

Or a private, cozy meal with a lover.

Jeez, where's your head at? Cooper snapped inwardly.

He turned his attention to the man across the table, who was studying him so intently he had the unsettling feeling he should have been paying much more attention to the guy.

"She's a special lady," Roger said.

"Yes," Cooper said automatically. And had the feeling the man knew it was a reflexive answer.

"She's had some tough times. I'd hate to see her go through any more."

Cooper had to make a quick decision. The chance of finding

out why she was so jumpy, versus possibly ticking this guy off and blowing his chance to get off that damned offshore mooring.

Live with it, he told himself. This was more important. Besides, what she'd said earlier this morning still haunted him. *Safety is an illusion.* He wanted this over, he wanted her to know and oddly, he wanted to be the one to tell her.

Not your job, he reminded himself.

"Tough times?" he asked.

"Yes."

The man simply stared at him, and Cooper suddenly realized his words had been a warning. The man was protecting her. Cooper wasn't sure what Roger thought his motives were, but just the fact that he cared enough to warn off a stranger told him a lot about the man himself. And while Roger was a generation, maybe two, older than himself, he looked tough enough and fit enough to make it more than an idle threat. And there was an air about him that said ex-military, or maybe even retired cop, the same sort of air his father's old buddies had. He'd seen enough of it; they'd been part of his life ever since his father had died.

"I don't know her that well," Cooper said, not sure what else to say. "Just from coming in here since I got here last week. So it was really nice of her to ask you to talk to me about the berth."

"You some kind of boat bum?"

"I work for a living." *Sporadically,* he added silently. "I just live aboard."

"Why?"

Odd question, he thought, but this was the man with the dock. And it was at his home, so Cooper supposed he had every right to be picky.

"It's important to me. The boat was my dad's."

"Was?"

"He's dead."

He said it bluntly, harshly, determinedly. He did that whenever it came up, which after all these years wasn't, thankfully, often. But even after more than fifteen years, he let the claws dig deep; getting over the pain would be like forgetting, and he didn't want to ever forget.

Roger just looked at him for a long, silent moment, and Cooper had the feeling the older man was seeing much more than just the insouciant, careless demeanor he projected. He would do well, he thought, not to underestimate this man.

Or the woman who chose him as a friend.

He wondered if she'd been looking for someone to take care of her high-maintenance self. If so, perhaps she'd found him. He thought of the leggy blonde in the photograph. That woman, maybe. The one across the room right now, doing what the blonde would likely think of as the most menial of work, and doing it with efficiency and flair and no sign of resentment, not so much. She didn't seem the type to look for anyone to take care of her.

So which image was wrong?

He'd glanced at her as the question formed in his mind, but now looked back. Roger was staring at him again, in that assessing way.

"Your father died young?"

"Far too," he said shortly. It wasn't something he discussed with anybody easily, let alone total strangers.

"How?"

Cooper grimaced. "He was a cop. Killed in the line of duty."

The man's gaze narrowed. What was he, some sort of cop-hating wing nut? Cooper wondered. There were places they abounded, he knew, those people who never made the connection that the very cops they hated were what enabled them to do their hating in peace.

"How?" Roger asked again.

That did it. He truly didn't talk about that. "What does this have to do with you renting me the dock space?"

"More than you might think," the old man said.

Cryptic. He hated cryptic. It always involved guessing, then got tangled in motives and worse, emotions, and your chances of interpreting all that right were marginal. His mother told him he was better at it than he thought, he just didn't understand the process and that made him scoff at it.

Your instincts are good, Cooper, she always said. *You just don't trust any conclusions that don't come out of some concrete process with evidence to back it up. Just like your father.*

Wow. The memories were running wild today.

To hell with it, he thought. The rowing was good for him.

"All I'm asking for is dock space. I'll pay you the going rate for a couple of weeks. In advance if you want it." *Thanks, Tristan,* he added silently. "I'll clean up after myself, shut down and be quiet at a reasonable hour we agree on. I won't do any damage, or if I inadvertently do I'll repair it." His mouth quirked. "And I won't bother you, or your home or steal from you."

He stopped, a little startled himself at the burst of words. He thought Roger almost smiled.

"I see," the older man said, and Cooper had the uncomfortable feeling the man did see more than he'd intended.

"That's the deal. It's up to you."

"And my tenant."

Cooper frowned. "I thought you lived there."

"I do. But I have a guest house."

"Oh. So I have to pass muster twice?"

"Would you mow my lawn?"

Cooper blinked at the non sequitur. "Mow…?"

"I'd rather tend my vegetables, and the fruit trees. Can't wait for the darn grass to die back for the winter."

Cooper resisted the urge to shake his head at this odd turn.

"Maybe you should turn it all into vegetables then."

"I could," the man said with a nod. "But my wife always

liked a nice, green yard. To chew it up after her death doesn't seem quite right."

Cooper's assessment shifted suddenly. Perhaps his earlier questions had simply been those of someone familiar with the death of a loved one to someone else in the same boat.

"Problem is," Roger said, "it's too big, and I'm tired of pushing that mower around."

"You should get a riding one."

"I've got one, but it hasn't run for a couple of years. And I figured the exercise was good for me."

"I could look at it, maybe get it going again."

"You're good with engines?"

"Tolerable." He hesitated, then looked up and met Roger's gaze as he added, "My dad was a good teacher."

There was a silent instant before Roger's eyes narrowed, and then he nodded. It was as close as Cooper could come to an apology for his earlier shortness, and Roger seemed to understand.

"You mow that blessed lawn, and get that riding mower running, I'll give you a week at my dock."

Cooper smiled. He couldn't help himself; the old guy reminded him of his uncle Marty, always dealing. "Never pay when you can barter," he always said.

"I might need more time," Cooper said,

"You can pay for that," Roger said. "Or I'll find something else that needs fixing. I've got a green thumb, but I'm all thumbs when it comes to things mechanical."

"Deal," Cooper said.

Roger nodded, and lifted his empty coffee mug in a gesture to Nell, who had filled everyone else's but left them to talk. But apparently she was watching, because she started toward them with the pot.

"You two reach an agreement?" she asked as she filled first Roger's, then his.

"We have," Roger said.

"All right," Nell said.

"Thanks," Cooper said, smiling at her. He took a sip of the brew, which was maintaining the quality that had directed him here in the first place.

"You're welcome."

The door opened for new customers, a group of six who had to be from warmer climes, judging by the way they were bundled up on this relatively mild day. Sheila, who worked the register and seated people, was on a break, so Nell was on her own for the moment. She glanced at him, then at Roger, and nodded. Then she left to go seat the newcomers.

Cooper set down his coffee mug and looked at Roger. "I guess the only thing left is to pass inspection with your tenant."

"You just did."

He frowned. "I just did?"

Roger nodded. Belatedly, it hit him. His head snapped around to look at Nell, who was leading the new group to a big table in the middle of the room with that practiced smile.

"Nell?" He looked back quickly, aware that in his chagrin he'd almost said *Tanya;* he'd better start thinking of her as Nell, or he was going to blow it. "She's your tenant?"

He should have guessed. Something about this case had screwed up his mind.

"She is. So in fact, I suppose you had already passed inspection, or she never would have suggested the idea to me. There are lots of people around here with dock space. And she's very…protective."

"And vice versa," Cooper said.

"Yes," Roger agreed easily.

It seemed the PI gods were smiling on him on this one, Cooper thought, forgetting for the moment about the weeks of drudgery that had gotten him this far. He'd found her despite the radical change in her looks, and now he'd landed literally in her backyard. He was going to be able to keep an eye on her and get some needed work done on *The Peacemaker* at the same time.

His only qualm was what her reaction would be when she found out he'd lied to her. Well, not exactly lied but certainly abridged the full story. He told himself not to worry about it. Once she saw her brother was alive and well, she'd be in a forgiving mood.

Why it mattered that she forgive him was something he didn't try to explain, even to himself.

Chapter 6

"This is a great place," Cooper said.

"It is," Nell agreed.

She watched as he went about tying up his boat with competent, practiced motions. "Nice boat," she said. "Roger said it was your father's."

He didn't really wince, but she knew that kind of pain too well not to recognize it, even in a split-second flash.

"Yes. And yes."

"I'm sorry. I know how hard it is to lose someone too young."

Roger had told her what Cooper had told him. The fact that his father had been a police officer killed in the line of duty had somehow eased her mind about him, although she supposed it was silly to assume that because the father had been one of the good guys, the son was, too. After all, it hadn't worked that way in reverse. Tris had been her rock, but their father had abandoned them long ago, and for all her understanding of why it had happened, and all the distance lent by time passed, the core pain never left her.

"But it's nice that you have it, that you keep it and take good care of it, in his memory," she said, meaning it. She wished there was something like that she could do for Tris.

He went still for a moment. He must be wondering what was up with her, she thought. This was the most personal thing she'd said to him, and it had to stand out after her aloofness.

"It is," he said, "the hardest work I've ever done, trying to keep it to his standards."

The admission moved her. "A perfectionist, was he?"

"About this, yes."

She knew a little about perfectionists. They could be hard—or impossible—to live with.

"Roger says a boat is a hole in the water that you pour money, time and, if you're not careful, your entire life into."

"That why he doesn't have one?" Cooper asked.

"Yes. He used to, but he gradually downsized so that now all he has is that little runabout, for fishing and crabbing."

Cooper looked toward the little fiberglass boat, maybe ten feet long, with a small trolling motor on it, pulled up onto the beach next to the dock.

"I should get one of those motors. Heck of a lot easier than rowing."

"Rowing's good exercise," she said.

"That's what I keep telling myself."

"It must be. You're in good shape."

For an instant he looked startled. What, did he think she hadn't noticed? True, it was only in the routine way people catalogued other people, in slots labeled *kid, adult, dog lover, lousy driver, quiet, boisterous,* whatever. But she'd have to be blind not to see that he was indeed in good shape. Rowing did amazing things for a man's shoulders, if nothing else.

"Passable," he said with a shrug of those shoulders.

He glanced up then, his attention obviously caught by something. She turned in time to see Roger coming outside the house and onto the small patio.

"Roger's owned this place a long time?" he asked.

"His family has, for about a hundred years. Used to be a working farm."

"You sure it still isn't?" he asked, glancing farther up the gentle slope toward what Roger called his garden.

She nearly laughed. It was a bit more than your average backyard vegetable garden with a fruit tree or two. She didn't know much about it herself, but even she could appreciate the variety Roger managed.

"It is amazing."

"This isn't the easiest place to grow vegetables," Cooper said. "With the short season and all."

"Roger told me. But he's got ways around it. A greenhouse, something he calls cold flats, cloches, other things. He starts very early so things are pretty healthy when he finally actually plants them."

"Where's your place?" he asked.

Her breath caught in her throat, and just that quickly the ease she'd begun to feel vanished. She could sense the instant panic coiling deep inside her, ready to be unleashed. She fought it down. It was a perfectly normal question. Just answer it, she told herself. He was going to be here, after all, and it's not like you were going to keep it a secret.

"Up there," she said, gesturing to the south side of Roger's house.

She saw him glance that way, apparently spot the corner of the little white building with cheery yellow trim, and nod. He went immediately back to coiling the excess mooring line into a neat circle on the dock, and she let out a long breath.

See? she told herself. Simple. Meaningless chatter between two people who didn't know each other but were suddenly going to be in close quarters for a while. She needed to rein in the paranoia. She'd opened this door by coming down here and talking to him, and it was going to look pretty odd if she slammed it shut now.

She thought she'd been ready. If she hadn't, she would never have even mentioned him docking here to either man. Or if she'd changed her mind, all she would have had to do was tell

Roger and that would have been it. And she certainly wouldn't have come down here when she'd seen his boat arrive.

"So, how long have you been here at Roger's?"

He wasn't even looking at her, he was lifting out a folding set of steps, for when the tide was in and the boat would ride higher. Nothing secretive or evil in the question, it was just more casual chatter.

"A few months."

"How'd you land all the way up here in Port Murphy?"

Suspicion spiked again. "What makes you think I haven't been here all along?"

He straightened up and looked at her head-on. His expression was puzzled. "Your tan?" he suggested.

She drew back slightly. "What?"

"People up here try, but it's hard, unless your budget runs to tanning booths," he said.

"Oh."

Well, there was a giveaway she'd never thought of. And she'd tried so hard to think of everything. Maybe she should have stayed at the same latitude instead of coming north.

But as Roger had once pointed out to her, half the people here had come from somewhere else. His own beloved Margo had been from Arizona, had forsaken the dry, sunny south for his sake, and had come to love the damp, mossy and beautiful northwest.

"You okay?"

She sighed. "Just thinking about Roger. And his wife."

"Oh, yeah, I meant to ask about that, so I don't say anything that upsets him. She died, I gather?"

Tanya nodded. "Ten years ago. They'd been married nearly forty years. More than half his life."

"Only thing I can think of worse is someone who's been there all your life," he said.

She froze. The panic uncoiled, struck. Her gaze shot to his face. This time he was looking at her, so intently it was as if he'd expected some sort of reaction.

"All your life." Like Tris.

Involuntarily she backed up a step, away from him. God, she'd made a horrible mistake. Jeremy *had* sent him, and she'd invited him here. She was such a fool, falling for... what? He was good-looking enough, but she was pretty much immune to that; Jeremy was considered by most to be a very handsome man. He seemed the polar opposite of Jeremy's driven ambition, bumming around on his boat, had that done her in? Or was it the cop thing, foolishly trusting him because of what his father had been?

He'd been speaking again, and she belatedly tuned back in.

"...how I felt when my dad died. It was like the world had literally crumbled around me."

He'd been thinking of his father? She felt an odd shakiness inside, the aftermath of the spike of panic-induced adrenaline.

"He was my hero," Cooper added simply, and that quickly her fear and suspicion died away. Could a man who could speak with such open love and admiration of his father be a bad guy?

"I'm sorry," she said again, meaning it. "How long ago was it?"

"A long time. I was fourteen."

Almost half *his* life, she guessed; he looked thirtyish. Even younger than she'd been when her mom had died. Degrees of loss, she supposed, didn't really matter much; when you loved someone the pain was too horrific to bear. "That's awful."

"It was."

He looked down at the dock, then up the hill toward the house, then at the water. As if he could look anywhere but at her.

"I'll let you get settled in," she said, when it seemed clear he wasn't going to say anymore.

He gave his head a little shake. "Thanks. I've got a couple

of things to do before dinner." He gave her a sideways glance. "You know Roger invited me?"

She hadn't. "Lucky you. He's a great cook. And he loves cooking for guests."

"Will you be there?"

"It's not our night."

He blinked. "Your night?"

"Sundays. I usually eat with him on Sunday nights. That's when he misses Margo the most. I think it helps, the distraction, I mean."

"Having a pretty woman around would do that," he agreed.

She gave him a narrowed look. And here he'd been being so sincere. But if there was anything she was sure of, it was that she'd successfully buried any trace of the glamorous woman she'd once been. Pretty had long vanished, and she knew it, was pleased with her new cloak of plainness, for more reasons than she would ever have imagined.

Still, the obviously false flattery stung, for reasons she didn't want to think about.

"He'll have to try that sometime," she retorted. She turned on her heel and left him there, not even bothering to look back.

Chapter 7

Ouch, Cooper thought, as he watched her stride away.

He should have left out the "pretty," he supposed. He hadn't meant anything by it. And he hadn't—he swore he hadn't—been thinking of the woman in the news photo. A shallow, carefree goof-up he might be, but he hadn't been trying to flatter her, win her over with meaningless compliments. It had just been a phrase that rolled out.

Nice. Yeah, that's what he should have said. A nice woman, instead of a pretty one.

But then again, he wasn't sure *nice* applied. Touchy, edgy, prickly....

Of course she's nice, he told himself. She wouldn't have done this otherwise, would never have even talked to Roger about letting him stay here. He was, after all, a stranger, no matter how much he might know about her.

Out of the corner of his eye he saw her pause in her journey up the slope, saw that Roger had started down and they'd met halfway between the edge of the small patio and the water. They chatted for a moment—Cooper wondered if she was telling the old man he was a jerk—and then each proceeded on their way, she toward the little yellow-and-white building, he continuing this way. Coming to check on the new tenant, no doubt.

Cooper had meant to just say hello and to thank the man again, but instead the first words out of his mouth were, "I didn't mean to make her mad."

Roger lifted a graying brow. "Did you?"

"She didn't say anything?"

"Nell has a lovely knack of keeping her own counsel. If she's upset with you, she won't tell the world."

"Oh." He gave the man a sideways look. "Why would being called pretty upset her?"

"Ah." The man said it as if he saw much more than the simple question revealed. "Perhaps because she works very hard at not being pretty?"

Cooper blinked. He'd better take care around this guy, he was obviously perceptive as well as smart.

"She could, of course, be stunning if she wanted to be. That bone structure wouldn't require much enhancement. So obviously, she doesn't want to be. I find that very telling in a woman."

Cooper stared at the man, wondering what kind of life he'd led that had made him such a…philosopher.

"Bone structure?" he said, seizing on what had struck him the most in the man's assessment.

Roger chuckled. "Sorry. Once an engineer, always an engineer, I suppose."

Cooper couldn't help it: he smiled at the man. Dinner conversation, he thought, was going to be interesting.

"So, as an engineer," he said, striving for a casual tone, "would you consider Nell high maintenance?"

The man looked shocked. "Nell? Hardly. She works too hard, six days a week. She doesn't go anywhere, except to the library, or drives with me to the grocery store on her one day off."

For some reason that relieved him, that walking a couple of miles laden with bags was a bit much, even for her.

"There's not even a television in her place. I offered to get one for her, but she said she didn't miss it. She comes up and watches a movie with me now and then, but otherwise, she does without."

"Kind of an austere lifestyle," Cooper said.

"Yes. She deserves so much better. I don't know why she does that to herself."

I do, Cooper thought.

"That's why I invited her to join us tonight. I hope you don't mind."

"Of course not," Cooper said, pleased he wasn't going to have to make sure she was where she was supposed to be without making the older man wonder what he was up to.

Although, after sitting down to what looked like the great meal she'd promised it would be, Cooper wondered if it would have been much different if she hadn't been there; she barely said a word. She'd bustled around between the kitchen and the patio, helping, but staying clear of what was obviously Roger's domain. And when he'd offered to help, she'd rebuffed him with a short shake of her head.

Still mad? He wasn't sure. But when she came back from one of her runs to the kitchen and seemed startled to find him setting the table with the silverware she'd brought on the last trip, he decided to find out.

"I know you think I'm an insensitive, ill-mannered jerk, but I can set a table. As long as there aren't more than two forks, anyway," he added wryly.

Her gaze shot to his face. After a moment, a small smile curved her mouth. And that *pretty* that had upset her, in that moment, seemed to apply.

"I never thought you were a jerk," she said.

As she let the *insensitive* and *ill-mannered* stand, clearly intentionally, an echoing smile broke out on his own face.

"Point taken," he said.

Her smile widened, and suddenly they were okay.

She set down the plates she'd brought, then glanced warily

at the sky to the west. Clouds were piling up behind the Olympics, dark and ominous. The first real storm of the fall was on its way.

"Roger said it's getting close to the end of being able to eat outdoors, so he wanted to. But I don't know," she said, eyeing the building clouds.

He looked, assessing height, distance, winds. "It'll hold long enough," he said.

She looked at him. "How can you be so sure?"

"Years of living with it."

"So…you grew up here?"

"Yep." It was the first question she'd ever asked him about himself, and she'd hesitated doing it, so he answered quickly and as cheerfully as he could. "On the other side of the sound, but still close."

"So maybe you do have roots after all. They're just wider spread than most."

He blinked. Opened his mouth. Shut it again. Stared at her. Finally managed to speak. "I never thought of it like that. But you're right. I love this area. Not that there aren't problems, but I can't imagine living anywhere else."

"So how did your mother end up in Spokane?"

"The rain finally got to her. I went to school at Wazoo in Pullman, and she came to visit a few times. Too hot for me, but she loved the warm and dry enough to put up with the colder winter. So she retired there."

"She never…remarried?"

"No."

He glanced up as the door opened and Roger came out bearing a huge platter of smoked salmon, three different cheeses, crackers, fried sweet potatoes still warm from the oven, and a large dish of sliced apples and a dipping sauce. Cooper guessed the fruit was fresh from his own trees; the garden was as much orchard as vegetables, and he'd noticed a couple of late-bearing trees among them.

"Maybe I should set her up with Roger. She might come back to the rainy side."

"Who might?" Roger asked, hearing the last words.

"My mother," Cooper said. "She's a strictly meat-and-potatoes cook, because that's what my dad wanted."

"This is, in essence, meat and potatoes," Roger said. "Just with a little more flair."

Cooper laughed as they sat down. "She'd love to learn to cook like this."

"Maybe you should teach, Roger," Nell—Cooper had successfully begun to think of her by that name—said, teasingly but with an undertone of seriousness.

"Oh, nobody'd want to take lessons from an old man who does nothing but putter around in his own kitchen."

Cooper had taken his first bite, flavor exploding across his tongue. He shook his head. "Feed them first," he said. "Then anybody with taste buds will sign up."

Nell gave him a startled look, then shifted back to Roger. "That's a great idea. Start with the garden club, fix lunch at the next meeting, show them what can be done with their edibles. You'd have a full class in no time."

Roger looked thoughtful, while Cooper processed how quickly she'd seized on his casual idea and turned it into a workable plan. Jones had told him she'd always been pretty much arm candy for Jeremy's fancy, fundraising functions, but she'd seen the potential here so fast it was clear she'd learned at least something.

It turned into a fairly lively meal, now that Nell had relaxed a little and participated. Cooper promised to take a look at the riding mower tomorrow, and get the yard—which was even bigger than he'd imagined—mowed as soon as it dried out from the oncoming storm.

He also picked Roger's brain about the motor on his little skiff; thanks to her brother, he could maybe afford one after this was over. Really, he'd landed in a patch of clover here. Because he'd happened to find her while her brother was halfway around the world, here he was, just killing time and getting paid for it until Jones could get here from London.

"So how did you end up here?"

He wondered if she'd answer this time. She'd cleverly avoided any discussion of where she'd come from before, but now she was more relaxed, and with a couple of glasses of wine, more loquacious. Especially with Roger here. And it was, after all, a perfectly natural question.

"It's where the next bus was going," she said.

"Which is how we met," Roger said. "The farmer's market is held in the parking lot of the marine hardware store, where the bus stop is. Lucky day."

She looked at the older man affectionately. "What he's not telling you is what a forlorn, helpless mess I was at the time. He took pity on me."

"Compassion, my dear. And I've been paid back tenfold," Roger added, getting to his feet. "And I think we have just enough time to decamp before the wind starts."

"You go, I'll clean up," Nell said. "And you leave those dishes alone!"

Roger laughed and went inside. Cooper got to his feet and joined her in gathering the dishes and glasses and piling them on the tray Roger had delivered the food with. He whistled lightly as they worked, hoping it would keep him from talking; his dad had always said it kept him out of trouble by keeping him from saying things he shouldn't. There was no need to probe, to push. All he had to do was keep an eye on her and wait. That was all he was being paid to do. But the curiosity that made him good at this was raging, and he was having trouble fighting it down.

"So, you like it here?" Good, he thought, it came out just like someone proud of their home, hoping the newcomer felt the same.

"I do," she said, with just the barest of hesitations. "More than I ever thought I would."

"You haven't been through a winter yet, though," he said.

"That could change your mind, make you long for weather down south."

She dropped a fork. "Down south?"

He'd never expected such a benign comment to cause such a reaction. He quickly said, "Like Roger's wife. Arizona, wasn't it?"

"Oh. Yes." She picked up the escaped utensil.

He didn't think he was imagining her relief. "It doesn't seem like safety is an illusion here," he said, his voice as quiet as he could make it.

She stared at him as he repeated her own words.

"It's always an illusion," she whispered. "You think your world is safe. Then it's shattered. Again and again. Then you know. Illusion."

She grabbed up the last spoon and dashed for the door. Cooper just stood there looking after her, finding it oddly hard to breathe. He'd never seen or heard anyone so devastated since the day they had buried his father and his mother had held on by a thread to get through the ceremony.

Finally, the first drop of rain hit the back of his neck and prodded him into grabbing up the heavy tray and heading for the house.

Chapter 8

It had just been casual conversation, that was all.

She'd lost track of how many times she'd told herself. She tugged at the comforter, pulling it up over her shoulders and she tried again for sleep. There was a chill in the night air now, promising more to come, but she liked the fresh air, so she left the window open and relied on the down comforter to keep her warm.

It was useless—her mind was still spinning. Out of that whole two hours over dinner, only at the end had he said anything that made her nervous. And that was just her, wasn't it? It was just her private knowledge that made her so edgy, so wary of the least little thing. His questions would be perfectly ordinary if she was just a person who'd landed here innocently. It was her own fear, her own history, that made them stand out, made them seem nefarious.

She rolled over again, warm enough now but seemingly unable to get comfortable. More than her composure had been rattled tonight. She couldn't deny the jolt of fear he'd caused in her when the questions had turned personal. When he'd thrown her own words about safety back at her, she'd nearly panicked. And she wasn't even sure why, just that she didn't like anybody paying that close attention to what she said.

And that comment about down south…had he really meant Arizona? Or someplace farther west? Had he been trying to get her to give something away? Why else would he spend so much time talking to her?

That was the crux of it. Why would this stranger show such an interest in a frumpy, boring waitress? Was there something more to it than simple politeness, trying to draw the third wheel at the table into the conversation?

In other words, was she going to have to pack up her few possessions and move on?

She was surprised at the stab of pain that thought caused. She truly, genuinely, liked it here. She even liked the life she'd built here. She had found things to like about her job, and enjoyed the challenge of being the most efficient she could be at it. She still had to find the balance between friendly openness and secrecy, but she was working on it.

And she adored Roger. He'd taken her under his wing the moment she'd arrived. She'd been wary of him at first, until she'd learned he lived here all his life, as had his father, his father's father, and so on, for over a century. No chance he would have had any contact with Jeremy.

Jeremy.

Her eyes popped open and she smothered a shiver as she stared into the dark. She sat up sharply, and reached over to flip on the bedside lamp. Light flooded the room, familiar now, a haven, and the urge to burrow deep and stay was strong.

She didn't want to run. If only because she had no idea where to go from here. East? Lose herself in the vast crowds of New York? Would that even be far enough? And how could she do it without being tracked? Jeremy had many contacts in the moneyed halls of most big cities.

Alaska, she thought grimly. Could she do that? She almost immediately discarded the idea; crossing the border would be a nightmare, and Jeremy had enough pull to have gotten her on some sort of watch list. She'd never make it. Unless she went by boat and avoided that part altogether. But short of hiring on on some fishing boat, as if they'd hire her, or paying some private yacht owner to ferry her up there and keep it quiet.

And just like that she was back to the man with the boat. She couldn't seem to get Cooper Grant out of her mind. Even when he wasn't asking her nervous-making questions, she'd found herself studying him throughout dinner. Noticed that he'd talked to Roger just as much as her. She liked that, that he paid attention to the older man, with every evidence of interest.

In that, he was like her brother. Tris had always had a genuine interest in others; he liked to talk to them, find out about them, why they were, where they were, who they were and where they wanted to go.

In fact, she thought, he reminded her of Tris in other ways, too. He had the same demeanor, that carefree attitude about life and responsibility. "Life's for the living, little girl. If you spend all your days worrying about what might happen, you never enjoy what *is* happening," he'd always told her. She, being the serious one, had sometimes despaired of that attitude in her beloved brother.

And sometimes, she had envied it.

Yet when the chips were down, Tris was always there for her. He always came through, he'd been the one she knew would ever and always have her back. He was the only one who'd known the truth, and he'd never, ever so much as doubted her.

Tears threatened, and now, alone in her quiet room, she didn't try to fight them back. Her brother was gone, dead and cold, and the sooner she accepted that the better off she'd be.

As for accepting that she was responsible for his death, she didn't know if she'd ever be able to do that. Her gut knew it, deep down, but her heart screamed in agony at the thought. And Tris wasn't here to tell her that even if it hurt now it would be okay later. Because it wouldn't be. The one man she had been able to rely on completely was gone.

Cooper Grant? Not likely. She didn't know if there was anything solid beneath the devil-may-care surface. And she wasn't about to trust him enough to try and find out.

She looked, Cooper thought, as tired as he'd thought she would. She'd answered the door quickly enough that he knew she'd been up and dressed, but he'd seen her light on in the dark hours before dawn.

He'd thought about going to her, telling her that he couldn't sleep, either, and that they might as well not sleep together. The unintentional double-entendre had made him groan aloud to the chilly night air, and he'd retreated to his stateroom, knowing if he was tired enough to even think stupid things like that, he was tired enough to make some big mistake with her.

"You're tired," he said, as she looked up at him a little blearily.

"Thanks for noticing," she muttered.

She reached a hand up as if to rub at her eyes, then caught herself. He didn't know much about contacts, but guessed rubbing your eyes with them in wasn't a good idea.

Without the heavy glasses, she looked quite different. Still not the blonde bombshell from the photograph, but different. This close, and without the dark-rimmed distraction, he could see the very faint edge of the colored contact lenses. He wondered for a moment if she ever left the glasses off, took the contacts out, and looked in a mirror just to see her real eyes again.

"I only meant I saw your light on last night," he said, wondering why he couldn't seem to even talk to this woman without antagonizing her.

"Sorry," she said. "I am tired."

"And it's your only day off," he said.

Her eyes narrowed, and he felt a spark of irritation. What the hell was wrong with her? She acted like every little bit of her life was a state secret. Maybe this was what her brother had meant by high maintenance. He was beginning to understand.

"I just wanted to be sure you were awake. I got the mower running, and I was about to start."

"Oh." She had the grace to looked chagrinned. "Thanks for checking."

"Sure. Hope I don't drive you away."

She gave him a sideways look, as if she were trying to figure out if he meant that on more than one level. He didn't help this time, just returned her look steadily, silently. Odd, he thought, he was finding her constant wariness wearing. Especially when he couldn't figure out the reason for it.

She probably needs a therapist, he told himself. Moving a thousand miles away, changing not just your surroundings but your entire life, was one thing that he could understand; he'd thought about it more than once himself in his own grief. But totally changing your appearance and jumping at every human contact seemed over the top.

When he finally headed toward the garage where he'd left the mower that a new spark plug and belt had fixed, he was no closer to an answer to the puzzle that was Nell Parker/Tanya Jones Brown than he had ever been. But at least she'd said she would be here all day, as usual, so he felt he could go about keeping his promise to Roger.

Once he had the feel and rhythm of the mowing process down, it was oddly soothing. It also didn't require a lot of thought, which left him too many brain cells to ponder puzzles. It was a good thing, he thought as he made the far turn on the now-purring lawn tractor, that part of this job wasn't to get Nell to trust him. Because he had no idea how to do it.

He glanced over his shoulder; he was down to one wide swath and he'd be done. He'd never mowed a lawn so big before. It had taken him nearly two hours, with the slopes and trees; he couldn't imagine what it would take with a push mower. He was thankful Roger didn't want the cut grass raked and bagged as well, or he'd be at it all day.

He had mowed carefully around Nell's cabin, not wanting to damage the flower beds by the door. Roger had said his green thumb didn't extend to flowers, so Nell must take care of these herself. And well, he thought.

And there he was, back wondering about the woman who had landed him here. And that little matter of trust. How did you get someone to trust you when it seemed they were on the verge of panic every other moment? He didn't usually have a problem with that. People tended to trust him, like they had his father. Women, especially. His mother's best friend, a wise woman he admired, had once told him it was because he was good-looking, but not so breath-stealing that they assumed he was a conceited jerk. He'd appreciated the feminine take on it. And women did seem to like him, and think he was a nice guy.

He *was* a nice guy, he told himself. There was no reason for Nell to distrust him, specifically. The knowledge that she did—and every instinct he had screamed it—gnawed at him.

He hadn't set out to charm anyone so resistant to him since snooty Serena next door when he was thirteen. He wasn't sure what it said about him that that, too, had been for a less than honest reason; a stupid, adolescent reason, a bet that he could get her to invite him on her family ski trip.

He'd lost that bet, but only because he'd quit on it. Crazily, he'd come to actually like Serena, especially once he'd realized she wasn't stuck up at all, but simply shy.

And amazingly, she'd come to like him, even after he'd told her the truth. He would have liked to have avoided that, but his mother had somehow found out about the bet and was so furious she'd made him do it. His mother was a formidable woman when angry, and not doing as she said wasn't an option. Besides, he knew his father would back her up, he always did.

And then a year later, his world had fallen apart, and Serena had been there for him in a way that had pounded home the lesson about never assuming that outward appearances were the whole truth.

This would be a finer dance, because he had orders to do nothing but keep track of her. But her brother wasn't even on his way yet, so he might as well do something to make it more interesting. After all, his natural curiosity was why he was in this business.

His mouth quirked. He was piling up quite a stack of reasons to do what he wanted to do. They were beginning to sound a bit phony even in his head. He might as well admit it all boiled down to one thing: the woman intrigued him. He wanted to know the whys behind what she'd done, taking off like that, changing her looks so drastically.

Maybe she was just crazy with grief, or maybe not. His gut was telling him there was more to it, and he wanted to know what. And if he had to charm her to find out, that was what he'd do.

Chapter 9

Tanya, she of the old life, had been used to attentive men. Not that she believed any of them. While she knew her looks perhaps made it less painful for them, she also knew too well it was her husband they were really after, and thought currying favor with her would get them to him.

Little did they know, she thought, as she inserted the contact lenses into eyes that were protesting after another night of too little sleep. Jeremy thought about as much of her opinion as he thought of anyone's other than his own.

But she wasn't in that life any longer. She wasn't that woman any longer. A glance in any mirror reminded her of that.

And a look in the mirror now showed her a very tired woman. The reflection she saw told her that brown or blue, her eyes were showing the signs of this string of restless nights. And the contacts weren't helping much. She hated wearing them, but they had seemed like a good idea at the time, and stopping now would require more explanation than she wanted to give to anyone.

She heard a distant whistle, a light, cheerful, meandering sort of tune. Cooper was up. It was odd, she'd never known anyone who whistled, really whistled, before. But he did, cornily, while he worked. Sort of absently, as if he weren't really thinking about it, as if it was just something he did while he was concentrating on something else.

If he ran true to the pattern established for the last week, he would show up at her door momentarily, ready to walk to work with her. She'd been beyond startled the first time.

"Coffee," he'd said. "Need coffee. Badly. You're going. I'm going."

Something about the short, choppy sentences, punctuated by a serious yawn, had made her smile as she accepted the unassailable logic.

"We could ride my bike," he'd suggested hopefully as they passed the motorcycle now parked on one side of Roger's driveway.

She'd cringed at the idea then, and shook her head. But this morning, she might just welcome the lift; she truly was tired. And since it was his fault...

It was a measure, she supposed, of how far she'd retreated into a protective shell that when he did knock on her door, it took everything she had to suggest it.

"That ride to work you mentioned," she began after the half-mumbled greetings that had become the norm; he was clearly not a morning person. Which made her wonder why he bothered to get up this early when he didn't have to. It wasn't like boat bums punched a clock.

But her words made him brighten. "You want a ride? Really?"

By the time they walked over to where his bike was parked, she was having second thoughts. She stood there looking at the shiny, black machine and wondered if she'd lost her mind. Walking would be better. It would wake her up. It would get her blood moving. It would—

"You've never ridden a motorcycle before, have you?"

"That obvious, huh?" she muttered.

"Pretty much, yeah," he said.

She realized she'd been eyeing the thing somewhat balefully. She tried for a smile, but was sure it was somewhat weak.

"It'll be all right," he said, his voice surprisingly gentle. "Give it a chance. You may love it. And if you hate it, well, you never have to do it again."

She looked at him curiously. "Do you love it? Or is it just the only way to have wheels when you're on land?"

"Can't afford a car in every port," he quipped. "But I do love it. Especially on a good, open road, one with some curves and tilt."

The image that conjured again almost made her change her mind. But before she could speak he reached out and grabbed the helmet that was strapped to the bike, undid it and handed it to her.

"What about you?" she asked, taking it reluctantly.

"Passengers always get the headgear," he explained. And then he grinned at her. "Besides, it's a good excuse to skip it. Nothing like riding free."

"Isn't there a law?" *Against that grin,* she added to herself. It could cause skipped heartbeats all over the place.

"I like living dangerously now and then," he said.

She knew a thing or two about living dangerously, and didn't see the appeal at all. But she felt committed now. Unhappily.

"Two miles," he said. "And if it freaks you out too much, I'll stop and you can get off."

That seemed fair enough. What could happen in two short miles?

Moments later, as she strapped on the helmet, she was again second-guessing her decision. And remembered wistfully the days when she hadn't worried about such things, when everything hadn't seemed fraught with peril.

You could always go back to the days when all your decisions were made for you, she told herself sharply.

The mental chiding worked. At least, until she was astride the bike behind Cooper and she realized just how close they were going to be. And that he was bigger, stronger, than she'd realized.

Calm down, she told herself. After all, what could happen

on a motorcycle? It wasn't like he could take his hands off the controls and grab her.

But she also hadn't realized she was going to have to hang on to…him. But this was a small bike, not one of those big ones with a separate, cushy backseat. And she was pressed against him like a lover, because she had no choice.

His matter-of-fact tone as he instructed her to keep her feet on the pegs he lowered, and to lean when he did, helped somehow. He put her hands decorously on his waist, with no urging to hold tight or jokes about the side benefits of a female passenger.

Idiot, she told herself. *Why would he? You're nothing special, and that's the way you like it. You—*

The roar of the engine beneath her as he fired up the bike made her heart jump, cutting off her thought. And as they started to move, all thought seemed impossible.

They started out slow, as befitted Roger's quiet street and the early hour. But once they were on the bigger, two-lane street, he picked it up a little. Instinctively her grip on him tightened, she couldn't help it.

It was the Monroes' red barn that did it. In a car, it was just sort of there, but now it leaped out at her, all of it, vivid and bright without the interference of metal or glass.

She drew in a deep breath to steady herself. Caught the scent of trees, of earth, with a touch of the approaching fall flavoring it all. Something she savored on her walks, but never would have noticed in a car.

Okay, so maybe she understood a bit of the appeal.

Then they hit the main highway, and he opened it up. Or at least, it seemed like it to her. And she realized with a jolt of fear that they'd never discussed *how* she could tell him if she freaked and wanted off. It wasn't like normal conversation was possible.

She tightened her grip, barely managed not to close her eyes. But after a moment she began to realize it wasn't so bad. And she'd thought she'd get cold in the chill morning air, but warmth was beginning to rise from the bike beneath her. And Cooper himself served as the perfect windbreak, and if she drew herself in behind his broad shoulders, she wasn't really cold at all. That realization distracted her enough to think about the sounds, the smells, the sense of speed and the hyperawareness of the road itself. And the odd sensation that was building in her, filling her.

On the next curve she leaned as instructed without even thinking about it; she had the rhythm of it now. And she thought of what he'd said, about a road with curves. She could see that now, the appeal of the constant shift and adjustment as you took each turn. You didn't just sit there and steer, your whole body was involved.

When he pulled to a halt in front of the café, much sooner than she'd expected, she was almost disappointed. Energy was surging through her, even more than after her usual two-mile walk here.

It took her a few moments to realize it was exhilaration she was feeling. And she couldn't remember the last time she'd felt this kind of heart-pounding awareness except in fear. It was more than a little shock to her, and she wasn't quite sure how she felt about it.

She fumbled with the strap-heavy helmet for a minute with fingers that were oddly numb. Strangely, Cooper just sat there on the bike, not even looking at her, for a long, silent moment. Then at last he dismounted, and reached out to help undo the unfamiliar fastening. He lifted the helmet off her head. Took one look at her face and grinned. That damned grin again.

"I knew you'd love it."

She didn't bother to deny what was probably showing on her face. "I'm not sure *love* is the right word, but it certainly is…invigorating."

"C'mon, you loved it."

"Maybe. A little."

She flexed her fingers, trying to get them to move normally

again. He set the helmet down on the seat of the bike. Then he turned back. Reached out and took her hands. The contact startled her. Her gaze shot to his face, and she fought the urge to jerk away.

"Next time, relax a little."

"Relax?" She wasn't sure there'd be a next time, or that she'd ever really relax again in her life. "I didn't realize it was supposed to be relaxing."

"No," he agreed, "but it would be easier on me."

She frowned. "What?"

"I think I have your fingerprints dug into my ribs."

She flushed, backed up a half step. His hands, still on hers, tightened and kept her from going farther. Panic bubbled up inside her. It was silly, he was still grinning at her, he clearly had no ill intent, but she couldn't help it.

"Hey, I didn't mean to embarrass you. You did great."

She stopped herself from screaming at him to let her go. Barely. And then he did, of his own accord. He busied himself fastening the helmet to the bike. And that quickly, her panic ebbed. She had to stop this, she thought, judging every man by one. With an effort, she smiled at this one.

"Thanks for the ride," she said. "It truly was invigorating."

"You ain't seen nothin' yet," he drawled. "We should take a good, long run, where you can really get the feel of it. I'd say up to Olympic National Park, but we'd need a bigger bike, with two of us. I'll have to check out some local roads."

She nearly told him not to bother, it wasn't going to happen, but she was too stunned at the thought of actually doing such a thing, just for enjoyment, to get a word out. And then Riley was there, the keys to the café in hand. The wiry cook eyed her, Cooper and the motorcycle, letting off metallic noises as it cooled in the morning air.

"Go start the coffee, will you, Nell?" Riley said after he unlocked the door.

"Of course." She was glad for the chance to escape into work. She looked at Cooper. "Thanks again for the ride," she said politely, and darted inside to what suddenly seemed like a refuge.

Cooper started after her, but stopped when a strong hand gripped his arm. Surprised, he turned to look at the man standing there.

"That girl's been through a hell of a lot," Riley said, and there was no mistaking the undertone of warning in his voice. And something about the man's steady gaze, and the surprising strength of his grip, told Cooper he'd be wise to heed that warning.

"I know," he said, not trying to pull away. "I only intend to make that better. I don't want to see her hurt anymore."

Absolute truth, Cooper thought. It had been the truth since he'd found her. But somehow it seemed a bit more intense this morning. More personal.

After a moment of intense scrutiny, Riley finally nodded. "I'll hold you to that."

Cooper knew he meant it. Just as Roger meant it. There was something about this woman that inspired a certain protectiveness. Not that she was weak, or helpless, it was just that aura of pain, that look of fear that flashed through her eyes now and then. Any man, any real man, would feel the urge to ease that.

He wished Tristan Jones would get here and end her hell.

Or did he? Sure, he wanted her hell over, but when it was, his job was done. And he'd be moving on.

Or would he?

Cooper Grant shook his head as he followed Riley into the café, wondering what rabbit hole his mind had dived into.

Chapter 10

He'd been a little surprised when she said yes. He'd expected her to beg off, but after some gentle encouragement from Roger, she'd agreed. Maybe she'd had enough of spending her one day off holed up in her little house or helping Roger in his garden.

Or maybe it was the promise that Roger would fix a nice lunch for them to take on the proposed ride through the countryside. If Cooper had to guess, he'd go for the latter; Roger's meals were nothing to take lightly. He'd been a guest at two of them now, and he'd never eaten better. He didn't even give a silent apology to his mother; she knew her cooking was good and hearty, but plain, as his father had liked it.

But he was more surprised at himself. He'd made some routine preparations yesterday, after she'd said she'd come. He'd risked that she would, as had been the pattern every day, never leave the café once she'd arrived. He'd fastened on the saddlebags, which would carry that lunch, a small blanket and rain gear just in case the predictions of a nice day were wrong. He'd scouted the planned route, along the western edge of the Hood Canal. Then he'd taken the hour's ride to the nearest motorcycle shop and picked up a helmet for her, a smaller one that would fit better and be more comfortable. It was a bit extravagant for one day's ride, but he told himself her brother was in essence paying for it. Besides, she'd been worried about his lack of headgear. And that made him feel…he wasn't sure how that made him feel.

What he was sure of was that somewhere along the line he'd morphed into a guy excited about a date with a girl he really liked. Crazy as it was, fake as the date was, it was true; he was as revved up as he could remember being in a long time.

And he *did* like her. There was something about her quiet ways that got to him, and that made the rare moments when she would smile or laugh as precious as sun breaks on a gloomy February day. He found he had to remind himself of the glamorous blonde in the photograph. And when he did, he wondered if he would like her nearly as much. Tanya Brown was some golden ideal, but Nell Parker was real, genuine and down-to-earth in a way he wasn't sure golden girls like the one in that picture ever were.

And he was lying to her every minute.

Cooper shook his head at himself as he pulled on his boots, then the heavy leather jacket he rode in. This was a job, nothing more. And he was just doing that job as instructed. After all, her brother had the right to give her this good news himself. And after nearly eight months, he guessed another week didn't matter so much. But Cooper found himself hoping he could at least see the moment when she realized the nightmare was not only over but had never really been true in the first place.

And surely, once she saw her beloved big bro, she'd forgive him for lying to her.

He laughed inwardly as he headed up toward the little yellow-and-white house. Like he was going to matter to her one bit in the joy of that moment. She'd barely remember he existed. But still, he couldn't help but want to see her, for once, free of that haunted look, feel of the wariness and that edge of tension that always seemed to hum around her.

Then he would be on his way, mission accomplished, brother and sister reunited, and a nice chunk of change in his pocket.

On his way to where, he didn't know. But then, he often didn't. Maybe he'd just head out and fish for a while. Salmon season was still open, and while he wasn't a true devotee, he liked the routine and the slow, steady movement and the excitement of a catch. Not to mention the good eating after.

He was pondering that pleasant prospect when the door to the little house opened just as he reached it.

"Hi," she said.

"Morning."

He looked her up and down. Just to be sure she'd dressed appropriately; he'd told her to wear a windproof jacket, and boots if she had them, explaining she'd be the one riding with her feet and ankles near the hot exhaust pipes. Her eyes had widened, but she'd nodded. And had done as he'd asked; the jacket looked heavy enough and the boots were nice, looking like they were lined with sheepskin, which would keep her feet warm. And they were practical boots, with a flat, lugged sole that would be good for some of the walking he had in mind.

"Is this okay?"

Her quiet question jerked him out of the reverie he'd slipped into unaware after his assessment of the practicality of her attire. He realized with a little jolt he'd never seen her in anything but the jeans and Waterfront Café T-shirt or sweatshirt she wore for work. Today she was wearing a lightweight sweater that subtly showed the curves the baggy shirts usually disguised, and her jeans were tucked into the top of the boots. Somehow the whole look had been like a punch in the stomach. She looked lean, lithe and leggy, like the woman in the picture.

That disguise she'd adopted was damned effective.

"Fine," he said hastily. "Good. Ready?"

"Coffee first?" She held out a disposable cup he hadn't even noticed she had. "It might be nice if you could manage more than one-word sentences."

He nearly gaped at her. She'd never teased him before, not like that. He hoped it was a sign she was relaxing around him, at last. Not to mention it warmed him that she'd thought of it.

"It's from the café. I brought some home last night and brewed it up this morning fresh," she said, as if that was the reason for his silence. "I just thought you might want your usual dose."

"Sounds great," he finally said, skipping any explanation of the wild jumble of his thoughts that was slowing his answers and making him seem half asleep to her. There was no way he could explain it to her when he didn't even understand it himself.

He sipped at the coffee she handed him as they walked up to the big house. Roger was waiting for them, smiling widely as he handed Cooper the large bag he held. He'd had to explain to the older man that the picnic basket he'd wanted to use wouldn't cut it on the bike.

"I held off on the wine, sadly," Roger said.

Cooper nodded. "Wine and two wheels are never a good mix," he said.

Nell's gaze shifted from Roger to him. He felt as if she were assessing him, or what he'd said. What had she expected?

"If you want it, fine. You're not driving."

He realized he sounded a bit sharp, and wondered what it was about this woman that seemed to bring out this weirdness in him.

"I'll save it for dinner." She gave Roger a fond, sideways look. "If I know Roger, I'm sure there will be enough for leftovers."

The man smiled, and sent them on their way with a wave as he went back inside. They walked toward the bike.

"How do we carry—never mind," she started, then stopped as she spotted the saddlebags he'd added to the bike. He'd already filled one side with the extra weather gear, leaving one side free for the food. And it was going to take up all of the room, he thought as he rearranged some of the things to get it all to fit. He spotted cheese and crackers, and a couple of huge, well-wrapped sandwiches, probably made with Roger's home baked bread, and his stomach almost growled in anticipation. Food had never been much more than fuel to him, but he could get used to this.

"You know what it is?" he asked, as he at last closed up and securely latched the saddlebag.

"Not for sure, but I think there's prosciutto involved. I picked some up for him yesterday."

So that had been the stop at the grocery store after she left work yesterday, he thought. He'd hung back in the doorway of the hardware store across the street where he could have a view of both the front and back exits of the small market.

Her routine seemed so set he could probably forgo following her home from work. But he didn't want to have to report to his client that he'd found then lost her. And it had only been a week since he'd found her, after all.

Only a week. The undeniable knowledge made his brows furrow. He'd found her; his job was essentially accomplished. All he had to do was keep an eye on her until Tristan got here, and although he hadn't expected it to take this long, that aspect was proving easy enough.

So why was she taking up so much of his conscious thought that it seemed like much longer than a week that she'd actually been in front of him?

"Got anything else you want to put in?" He'd noticed she wasn't carrying a purse. In fact, now that he thought of it, he didn't think he'd ever seen her with one.

"No."

"ID, cell phone?"

"Back pocket, and don't have one."

He blinked. And he thought *he* traveled light.

He handed her the helmet he'd picked up for her. Her own brow furrowed. "Where did this come from?"

"The motorcycle shop in Port Angeles," he answered literally.

She blinked. "You bought a helmet? Just for this?"

"You said you wouldn't come unless I wore the helmet. And I wouldn't if you didn't. So."

"Aren't they expensive?" she asked, sounding concerned.

He found that interesting. Tanya Brown had certainly never had to worry about money, probably never even thought about the cost of things. Yet here she was worried about how much he'd spent on something protective for her. It was another of those tiny notes that clashed with the image of that woman in the photograph. And with what he'd been told.

"It's used," he said. "It wasn't that much. But it's in good shape. You'll be fine."

He wished he could have gotten her at least a leather jacket, but the only one they'd had had cost more than he had at the moment. He'd just have to make sure she didn't need it, he told himself.

Then, on impulse, he said, "You need the glasses for distance?"

Wariness spiked through her visibly. "Why?"

He shrugged. "Just be easier without them. On your ears if nothing else. Those frames are kind of thick."

She hesitated for a long, silent moment. And then, in a quick motion that made him think she was doing it before she could change her mind, she reached up and yanked off the glasses.

Answers that, he thought. She didn't really need them.

And removing them truly changed her face. They were so dark and heavy they almost overwhelmed her delicate features; he'd be willing to bet that anyone who just saw her once would later describe her as "the girl with the glasses." He wondered if she'd chosen those frames purposefully to draw attention there rather than to herself. She certainly hadn't chosen them because they were flattering.

She slipped the bright blue helmet on. It fit her much better than his had, he could see that immediately and so, judging by her smile, could she. She adjusted the D-ring strap quickly this time; she learned fast.

He picked up his own helmet and strapped it on. But he

wasn't thinking about it, he was thinking about her. As usual, of late. He supposed it was a measure of how much she'd loved her brother, how drastically she'd changed herself. And apparently more than just physically. She'd gone from living in a huge, gated mansion to a tiny cottage in someone else's backyard. From driving a high-end luxury car to walking to work. For that matter, from not working at all, probably just shopping to fill her time, to working as a waitress six days a week.

Oddly, she didn't seem angry about it, either. She just…did it. As if there were no choice, and no use in dwelling on it.

Finished with his own helmet strap, he turned to her. "Ready?"

The blue helmet bobbed. She was game, but still a little nervous; it showed in what he could see of her behind the face shield.

"Same deal," he said. "It starts to freak you out too much, you tell me and we'll stop. Eat lunch in a parking lot or something."

He couldn't see her mouth, but her eyes told him she was smiling.

"But how do I tell you?"

He was tempted to tell her to squeeze him harder, but decided that was just asking for trouble. Hell, the five-minute ride to the café with her snugged up tight behind him had played havoc with his senses—who knew what *this* would do? The only good thing about it was that ironic little voice in his head saying maybe he wasn't so shallow after all.

Or maybe he was just horny, he thought drily. It had been a while.

"Rap me on the head," he muttered, meaning it in more ways than she could possibly know.

Chapter 11

While this wasn't the worst mistake she'd made in her life—Jeremy won that title, hands down—it surely was the worst one since that life had ended. What had possessed her to say yes to this? Why had she thought clinging to this man, aboard this dangerous machine, was a good idea? If she'd wanted, on some level, to shake up her quiet little world, she'd certainly managed that. Her heart was pounding, pulse racing, as they leaned into another curve.

But she couldn't deny it was exhilarating. She had, as he'd promised, gotten the rhythm of it as they swooped first through the woods then down along the canal—really a fjord, he'd told her. She'd learned to anticipate the moment when he would lean into the next turn, and when he would straighten up after. She could sense the shift in his body a moment before, and had learned to move when he did. The sight, the sound, the smell, it all came together into a sensory experience she hadn't expected, and had never even come close to in her life.

He was obviously good at this. And maybe clinging to him wasn't really so bad. He was lean, and strong, and for the moment at least didn't seem like a threat.

At the moment, he's the only thing between you and a nasty crash, she thought wryly.

But that didn't seem likely. Nothing bad seemed possible just now; it was a glorious day, almost fall, with splashes of color from yellow to orange to explosive red beginning to show here and there against the backdrop of the evergreens, a crisp coolness in the air, but still with the warmth of the sun burning through. She'd grown up where there was little change in the weather from season to season—some joked California had seasons, it was just that they were fire, flood, earthquake and drought—and this was a novelty for her. And she liked it.

When they stopped at a state park along the water's edge, she was surprised. When she realized they'd been riding for forty-five minutes, she was stunned. It had seemed much shorter.

Cooper took off his helmet and, he said with a laugh, put on his tour guide hat. This park was unique, because it combined freshwater and salt, being at the mouth of a river running down from the Olympic Peninsula to empty into the canal. He'd obviously been here before, because as they walked along the tidal flats he told her all manner of fascinating things about the canal and its inhabitants, and he knew everything by name. Her mind was a blur of so many different birds, she marveled he could remember them. They could come back and do some clamming, he suggested; the season was still open for a little while yet.

By the time they sat down to eat Roger's wonderful lunch she was ravenous in a way she hadn't been in months. The cheese and crackers were subtle, almost delicate, and were followed by little cups of the shrimp salad he'd made the first time she'd eaten with him and had told him she loved. Trust Roger to remember that. The sandwiches were thick and delicious, layers of ham and cheese and other things full of flavors that exploded between slices of Roger's wonderful bread. A custardlike dessert topped with kiwi fruit was the perfect final touch. He'd cleverly packed it all with bottles of frozen water, which kept it all chilled while packed, and now served as drinks.

"I can honestly say I've never eaten that well in a restaurant, let alone on a picnic table and out of my bike's saddlebags," Cooper said.

"I can honestly say I've never eaten that *much*, ever," she said, almost ruefully.

"It's the open air," he said. "Plus, riding's more work than you might think. You don't just sit there, like in a car."

She'd seen that for herself, and nodded. After a moment he went on.

"Some go for the new stuff, synthetics, even Kevlar, like in bulletproof vests. But it's expensive, and some people are traditionalists and stick with leather."

"Like you," she said, looking at the heavy jacket he'd pulled off and laid on the end of the picnic table.

"It was my dad's."

His voice was quiet, and held an undertone she knew all too well.

"How did it happen?"

The question was out before she thought, and she almost wished it back the moment she'd said it. He drew in a deep breath, then let it out, slowly. She opened her mouth to apologize, to say never mind, but before she could he answered her.

"He walked into a convenience-store armed robbery."

"Walked in? You mean he wasn't sent there?"

He shook his head. "No. They hadn't called it in, it was literally in progress. The guy saw the uniform and panicked. Started shooting."

"How awful." She remembered what he'd just said about new motorcycle gear. "Wasn't he wearing a bulletproof vest?"

"Didn't matter. Round hit him in the neck. Severed his spinal cord. They say he probably never knew what hit him."

His voice was so bleak, so grim, she let other words she never meant to say slip out.

"My mother died slowly. Cancer. It doesn't matter, it's horrific either way." She barely suppressed a shudder. Memories of her own tearing, crushing grief when her mother had died nearly swamped her. "I'm sorry, Cooper. Really."

Her voice was a little shaky. He must have heard it, because he reached across the table and laid his hand over hers. His was warm, strong and somehow soothing. As if he knew just how she felt. And he did, she thought. They'd both been through the worst loss a child could have. Each horrible in its own way, yet different. Hers random, his random yet not really. Somehow his seemed worse: it had happened with intent, and to a man who served. Not that her mother—

She gave herself an inward shake. Her thoughts were getting jumbled. Because it was an emotional topic, she told herself. Not because he's touching you.

"I'm sorry, too," he said at last, his voice a little gruff. "If it hadn't been for me, he wouldn't have been there at all."

"What?"

"He traded shifts so he could go to my baseball game the day before. It should have been his day off. He died because of me."

Her breath caught. "Cooper, you can't seriously blame yourself? He just did what any loving father would do, to support his son, show him he loved him."

His mouth twisted. "If I had a nickel for every time I've heard that…"

She pulled back slightly, a bit stung by the words. And by the fact that he'd pulled his hand back. She instantly missed the warmth.

"I only meant—"

"I know what you meant. I know you meant well. It's just…" He stopped, ran a hand over his chin, then sighed. "When you're fourteen, none of that means anything. You're still pretty much focused on yourself, and everything that happens around you seems somehow be connected to you."

She absorbed that, saw the truth in it. "I guess your view at fourteen is still pretty narrow."

He nodded. And for a long moment he just looked at her. She

got the oddest feeling he was now thinking about something else entirely.

"He really was there because of me. And guilt, it does crazy things to you. Makes you do crazy things."

She knew a little something about that. And to her shock, Cooper Grant was looking at her as if he knew she knew. As if he somehow saw past the disguise to the truth behind it; unlike the boy he'd been, she'd been as responsible for Tris's death as if she'd pulled the trigger herself.

She shivered inwardly, reaching for the old pain to suppress the newer one.

"There's nothing like losing a parent," she said.

He put his hand back over hers. The little jolt she felt was like an alarm going off, but she barely noticed the warning.

"How old were you?"

"Seventeen. Almost an adult. But we were…really, really close. I thought the world had ended."

"In a way, it had," he said.

His quiet words were so different from the usual platitudes of *You get over it,* or *At least you had her that long,* that she found them oddly soothing.

"Yes. And after she died, my father…he completely lost it. He'd been with her since high school, and he simply couldn't live without her."

Cooper went very still except for his fingers, which tightened around hers. By now it seemed so natural she hadn't even thought of pulling away.

"Are you saying he killed himself?"

"I don't know. Probably. He just vanished one day. Left everything. Including my brother and I."

It hurt, to even mention Tris. And she was wishing she'd never started this.

"So you don't know?"

She let out a compressed breath. "Not really. We looked for years, my brother and I, but we never found him. And I spent the next five years trying to put it back together."

"Can't be done."

Again the simple acknowledgment was comforting in a way platitudes never were. "I found that out. Too late. I wanted to feel safe again. So I made…a big mistake."

He didn't speak, just waited. She was more than a little shocked that she was talking to him at all about this. But after he'd been so open about his father, after he'd said just the right things about her mother, it just seemed natural to trade confidences. Despite the warnings going off in her head, something about the way he looked at her, something warm and steady in his eyes, made it easier to talk than not.

"I married a man who made me feel that way again. Safe. He was charismatic, powerful and I felt like he could stand between me and the darkness."

He was looking at her so intently it was almost unnerving. It seemed more than simply paying attention to what she was saying, it was as if he were thinking rapidly, as if he were looking for some kind of answer in her words. Which nearly made her give a bitter laugh; she had no answers, she didn't think she ever had.

"What happened?" he finally asked when she didn't go on.

She didn't know if he'd chosen her own words purposely, to make her feel she had to answer as openly as he had. If he had, it worked.

"I woke up one day and realized I'd become…an accessory, polished up and kept on a shelf until he needed me for some display."

His gaze narrowed. She felt a spark of satisfaction as she guessed he was wondering what on earth was display-worthy of the plain little bird she'd become.

It was a sour sort of recompense for her efforts. She stood up and began to gather the few items to be taken back to Roger. He took them as soon as she had them together. She picked up the wrappings and discardable things and walked over to a garbage can and deposited them carefully.

When she turned back he was standing by the motorcycle, watching her, no doubt wondering why she'd ended the intense conversation so abruptly. Yet he didn't ask, didn't push. In fact, as she came up to him he didn't say a word.

"Thank you for today," she said, rather formally. "It's beautiful here. I haven't explored much since I've been here, but now I'd like to."

"It's not over yet," he said.

True, she thought, the ride back was yet to come, and although the days were getting noticeably shorter—another oddity to her, here in these northern latitudes—they still had a lot of daylight left.

When he turned off the main road shortly after they'd gotten back on it, she realized he'd had something more specific in mind. They were going along the river, she realized. Then after two or three miles, crossing over it. She'd barely had time to register that when he was pulling over and parking.

"Where are we going?" she asked after, at his indication, she pulled her helmet off again.

"You'll see," he said cryptically, and fastened both helmets to the bike.

He led her off the road, into the trees. He kept going to where a metal gate controlled vehicle access to a narrow track. He slipped past it. She hesitated, and he reached back and took her hand, tugging her after him.

She went forward a couple of steps, although she was wary. Then she spotted a small, cement block building. A windowless place, with a set of heavy double doors and a large power meter of some kind beside them.

She stopped dead in her tracks.

"Nell?"

He was looking at her in what seemed to be simple puzzlement. But he had a tight grip on her hand, as if to keep her from running. And that was exactly what she wanted to do.

The panic that was an old companion now flared, searing her into immobility. Visions of every kidnapping movie she'd ever seen flashed through her head. The shadowy woods, the isolation, the spooky, escape-proof-seeming building, it all looked like the perfect place to hide something.

Or someone.

All the nightmares she'd been living with for months seemed to coalesce into this moment. She wondered if this was it. She wondered if Roger's lunch had actually been her last meal.

And she wondered how long it would take for anyone to find a body buried in these woods.

Chapter 12

Cooper sensed the moment when she changed from curiosity to fear, but he had no idea why. She was pulling back, and he was holding on, trying to understand. True, the little hydro plant building wasn't particularly inviting, but they weren't going there.

"We have to go past this," he explained, as she kept trying to pull away. "The trail runs on the other side of it."

"Trail?"

"It'll be worth it, I promise. And it's not hard, or steep, or even very long."

"To where?"

"That's the surprise," he said.

For a long moment she simply stared at him, as if she were trying to see into his mind.

"Nell? What's wrong?"

This woman was going to make him crazy. And not only because her brief reference to her marriage bore little resemblance to what her brother had told him. She wasn't just skittish, she was downright spooked, and he couldn't figure out why. Some pieces he'd thought fit neatly together suddenly didn't anymore. He needed to think about this, but right now he just needed her to calm down.

"I know it doesn't look like much from here, but you'll like it. Trust me."

She looked at him as if nothing could convince her he was trustworthy. Some part of his brain was trying to understand how the admitted tragedy she'd fled had brought her to this; the fleeing all the memories he understood, but the fear made no sense to him.

She tried to pull away again, and this time he let go. He held up his hands. "Okay, okay. It's up to you. I'm going, you can follow, or not. But you'll miss something worth seeing if you don't."

He started around the hydro plant building, toward the almost hidden trail. He was twenty feet away before, finally, and hesitantly, she followed. He let out a relieved breath and continued on, although he slowed for her to catch up.

It had been a while since he'd been here; he only hoped he hadn't oversold it. Not after going through that little scene to get her there.

He pondered it as he walked, figuring silence was the best option just now; if he didn't talk, he couldn't scare her off, right? He supposed he didn't have to make sense of it, or her, he just had to keep her from bolting, from vanishing again. It didn't matter if he didn't understand why she would.

Except that she was afraid, and that bothered him. Not knowing why, or what he'd done to spark that fear, bothered him.

She bothered him.

He only needed to remember their conversation over lunch to pound that home. He so rarely talked about his dad, about what had happened and about the guilt he'd carried around ever since, no amount of telling himself it wasn't his fault, he'd been only a kid, able to ease it. Yet it had seemed to pour out of him, and he wasn't even able to tell himself it had been to get her to open up in turn, even if it had turned out that way, a little at least.

It hit him then, belatedly. He should have tumbled to it

sooner. Was that the simple answer for her wariness, her distrust? She had, in effect, been abandoned by both parents. Her mother by accident, her father by intent, which had to be worse.

He tried to think what his life would have been like if, after his father's death, his mother had done what Nell's father had done. Gone into a downward spiral and then disappeared. He couldn't even imagine it. He and his mother had clung together in the aftermath. If he had lost her, too…

And he thought he understood a little better now the depth of the bond between brother and sister. If they had drawn together as he and his mother had, it made sense that thinking she'd lost him, too, would be devastating. And if she truly felt that way about her husband, regardless of if it was valid or not, she must feel like everyone she cared about left her, in one way or another.

He'd been, he thought grimly, pretty thoughtless about it, all in all.

Story of your life, Grant.

He turned to look back at her. She was trudging along steadily, but still looking uncertain about the wisdom of it. They were close enough now he wanted her to focus on the ground, the trail, wanted her looking anywhere but up ahead.

"It may be a little slick from here on," he said quietly. "Watch where you put your feet."

And then he held out his hand to her. But this time he waited, leaving the decision to her.

Nell looked at his hand, remembered how he'd held it down by that scary little building, refusing to let go. She'd be a fool to take it again, wouldn't she? Except this time he was giving her a choice. All she had to do was say she'd be fine and keep walking. She sensed he would let it go.

But if she was right, and he would, then there was no reason not to take it, was there?

Lord, her mind was turning into Jell-O. Quivering and soft.

"I don't want you to get hurt," he said. "It's only a little farther."

She stared at his proffered hand. This somehow seemed like a much bigger decision than simply accepting some assistance over the occasional rock that was, indeed, rather slick. Everything was a bit damper now, more than seemed normal, simply from their getting deeper into big trees.

She'd come this far. If she'd been going to run, she should have done it back at the beginning.

Crazily, that made the decision—right or wrong—clearer, and she finally reached out and took his hand. He squeezed her fingers for a moment, as if he knew it hadn't been easy for her.

As if staring at his hand like it had seven fingers, or was covered in scales hadn't made that pretty clear, she chided herself when he proceeded to indeed simply help her the rest of the way.

Again he cautioned her to watch her feet, although to her it didn't seem the trail itself was bad at all. But what rocks there were were indeed wet and slick with algae, so she did as he said and concentrated on the trail. Still, she realized she was hearing something, a sound that grew nearer, a sound she recognized, but before she could put a name to it, Cooper stopped in front of her.

"Okay, you can look up now."

Startled by his words—had he been purposely trying to keep her from looking around?—her gaze shot to his face. And then he stepped aside, and she realized he'd been intentionally blocking her view.

What she saw made her gasp. A waterfall, at least a hundred and fifty feet high. Not a roaring, gushing torrent, but a tracing of countless little streams down a rocky face, making the whole almost delicate, ethereal. They flowed into a pool at the bottom, again no churning chaos but a calm, peaceful gathering of myriad trickles.

She stared, thinking she'd never seen anything quite like it, and certainly not such a short distance from a main road. It was beautiful, yes, but many other things, too. It seemed to scour out all the fear, the pain, and leave her, for just this moment, able to do nothing but take it in and let it fill her with a sense of wonder she'd not felt in a very long time.

He said nothing, just let her look, let her drink it in. At last she turned to look at him, feeling a complete fool for her earlier fears, all at the sight of a tiny, remote building.

"Thank you," she said, heartfelt.

"It's a lot fuller, more of a traditional falls later, when we've had more rain," he said, "but I like it now. It looks almost... intricate."

That told her a lot about him, she thought. She would have assumed most men would appreciate the roaring torrent over this almost delicate tracery.

"Not that Snoqualmie in full run isn't massively awesome," he said. "You stand on the observation deck and you can literally *feel* the power of it."

Okay, so he liked both. That told her even more, she thought.

The ride back to Roger's was just as exhilarating as the ride out. The difference was, she felt a niggle of regret that the wonderful day was nearly over. She felt as if the cloud that had surrounded her, wrapped her gloom for so long, had lifted, at least for this golden afternoon.

And she had him to thank for it. She felt sillier every minute for having been so afraid, thinking of kidnappers and killers when in fact he'd done one of the nicest things anyone had ever done for her. It seemed all too soon that he was parking the bike back on the edge of Roger's driveway.

"Thank you. That was wonderful."

He gave her that crooked grin that reminded her so of Tris. "Liked the waterfall, huh?"

"I loved it. But the whole time was wonderful."

"We'll have to take a run out to Snoqualmie, so you can compare. That's a couple of hours, though, but a great ride. Maybe your next day off?"

That he'd also enjoyed today, enough to suggest that, warmed her. As did the fact that he'd thought of that walk to the falls and, more, had wanted to surprise her with it, keeping her distracted until they were almost upon it.

Yes, she was an idiot. As if a man who would think to do that would be some crazed secret murderer, or be doing the bidding of a man like Jeremy.

"I'd like that," she said. "I haven't had a day like this in a very long time."

"Too long," Cooper said. "This is beautiful country, you should see more of it. It's a lot different here than…where? California?"

The old fear flickered, but failed to catch this time. Besides, it was safe enough, California was a very big state. And people left it every day. Lots of people. No reason to deny it, she thought.

"Yes. Only waterfall I've seen there is Yosemite."

That had been so long ago, in her blissfully ignorant childhood.

"Never seen that one."

"My parents took us one summer. We sort of camped, in one of those platform tent things. My dad cooked on campouts. My mom herded us but gave us a lot of slack, because it was a vacation."

She stopped, unable to believe she'd run on like that. She'd been hiding so long and so completely it felt almost like speaking a foreign language to talk about such things.

"Why'd you leave?"

The fear was a spark this time, brighter, closer to catching.

"What?"

"Sounds like you had a good life there."

"I did," she said, the old wariness back in her voice. "A great life. But everyone who made it great is gone."

He didn't give her the expected platitude, for which she was grateful; there was never an easy way to respond.

"Nell…"

There was a world of empathy in his voice, and if she pushed her imagination a little, it would be all too easy to interpret it as genuine caring. And then he stepped forward, took the blue helmet from her and set it on the bike's seat.

And put his arms around her.

Every bit of common sense she had screamed at her to pull away.

Every bit of yearning and longing in her made her stay.

He was strong, and warm, and at the moment tender, and the warmth she felt in his embrace was too tempting, too soothing. It couldn't hurt, could it, to just take this, for a moment? She could be allowed that much, in the cold, empty place her life had become, couldn't she?

She felt a slight pressure, realized his chin had come to rest atop her head. He said nothing, simply held her, as if somehow he knew words would be too much.

She didn't know how much time passed before she realized he was somehow sapping her strength. That somehow her legs were weakening, and she was leaning into him, as if her body had made a decision her mind was unaware of, to seek more and more of his steady, strong heat.

The fear roared to life this time, caught and flared. She had to get away. It was too much, the wonderful day, the crushing return to reality, and now this.

She pulled back. For an instant he resisted letting her go, as if he were savoring it as much as she had, which was possibly the most ridiculous thought she'd had all day.

"Thank you again." It came out stiffly, but she couldn't help it. "I have to go get ready for work tomorrow."

In fact she'd already washed her café shirts, they were ready to go, but it was the only thing her frazzled mind could come up with.

When she turned and left him standing there, it was all she could do not to run.

Chapter 13

Cooper stood in the main salon of *The Peacemaker,* trying not to pace. He needed to be still, because his mind was racing in so many directions at once.

He'd managed to make her relax. That was good.

Then he'd somehow spooked her on the trail. Not so good.

But she'd loved the falls. Good.

And the ride back. Also good.

Then he'd revved her back up with his questions. Not so good again.

Then he'd hugged her. Held her. For too long. And he had absolutely no idea where that fell on the good-not-so-good scale. All he was sure of was that his own fierce response to holding her had taken him by surprise. Who'd have thought the quiet little bird she'd become could spark that?

And what the hell was he doing, making plans with her for a week from now, when it was very likely he'd be long done with this job by then? Damn, he'd practically asked her on a date. A real one. And no amount of telling himself he didn't mean it, it was just part of the job of keeping her in sight as much as possible, seemed to be working.

He only realized he'd lost his battle to be still and think when he stopped pacing at the polished mahogany shelf where he kept his cell phone and keys. He'd turned the phone off today, not wanting any interruptions.

That should have been a clue you're out there, Grant, he told himself, as he picked it up and turned it back on. And as he did, he wondered why she didn't have a cell phone. There were pay-as-you-go phones that put them within reach of almost everyone. But maybe that was it—she didn't want to be within reach herself. Maybe it was part of cutting herself off completely from her old world, which she seemed so determined to do.

The world in which her brother was dead.

He realized he was pacing again, gave up trying to stop. Damn it, he wanted to tell her. The more he saw of her, the more bruised and battered and tormented he saw she was, the more he wanted to put an end to it.

He'd never had a sibling, so he really could only guess at that kind of love, but it was obvious she loved her big brother deeply. There was only a couple of years between them, Jones had said, and Cooper wondered if that made them closer.

And he could only imagine the bond between them strengthened immeasurably after they'd lost, in essence, both parents.

He understood, sort of. He'd been worried about his mother after his dad had been killed, and for a while had been afraid for her, at least as much as his fourteen-year-old mind could process her mood. She'd told him once, after a crying jag that had frightened him into thinking he was going to lose her, too, that she'd lived with this in her head for years, every cop's wife did.

Later, when he'd been a little older and he'd asked her about that time, she said being married to a cop, you always knew something like this could happen. It had been like having an abscess, always there, putting pressure on you, painful, and worse when you focused on it.

And when it had finally happened, it was like that abscess

that ruptured, draining its poison through her system, and it had been touch and go whether it would kill her, too.

She'd been safely past that point when he'd asked, although to this day she occasionally got teary eyed when she thought about his father. It had rattled him a little when she admitted she'd considered ending the pain. But she hadn't, because of him. She wouldn't, couldn't, do it to him, couldn't leave him, she loved him too much.

Yes, he'd been rattled, not only because of the close call, but because he realized he'd somehow sensed it, back then, even at fourteen. Just as he'd sensed when it was safe to ask, much later.

You're a perceptive kid, Cooper. And observant. You'd make a good cop.

His father's words shot through his mind, stopping his pacing midstride. He remembered it so clearly, that day on the way to the ball field. A woman had been leading a young boy away from the field where the younger Little League team had just finished a game. The woman was yelling at the child, chastising him soundly as she hustled him toward the parking area.

"She's pretty upset," his father had said.

"She's probably just scared," Cooper answered.

His father had looked at him curiously. "Why do you think that?"

Cooper remembered feeling a spurt of panic, because he wasn't quite sure why he thought it, and he didn't want his dad thinking he was stupid. It took him a moment to dissect the mental process that had happened so fast, and another moment to get it into words. But his father had waited, patiently.

"Because his shirt was torn, and he was bleeding a little. And she was pulling at him, but not that arm, she was real careful. And she was yelling at him about being careful. So I think he got hurt, and that scared her, and she yelled. Mom does that, sometimes, when I scare her."

And that had earned him the accolade that had swelled

him up with pride for weeks afterward. And filled him with determination to be just that, when he grew up.

And less than six months later his father had been dead.

His phone's message alert chirped, startling him out of the morass of memory. This was followed by another, different chirp declaring the presence of email; it had caught up after being off for so long.

The email was from his mom, a chatty, catching-up kind of thing, since she'd been off visiting his aunt Claire in Colorado for a week. He'd get to that later, he thought, as he checked voice mail. Two messages from his college buddy Derek about a pickup baseball game next week, one from the last woman he could technically call a girlfriend, announcing pointedly that she was engaged. And next came a text message from Tristan Jones. The man seemed suddenly addicted to them, never simply leaving a voice mail anymore. Cooper hadn't actually spoken to the man since the call after he'd found his sister. The message reported he was having trouble extricating himself from scheduled meetings, something about cabinet ministers, but hoped to be on his way tomorrow.

Cooper's mouth quirked as he exited the program and put the phone back on the shelf. Cabinet ministers? That was some job Tanya's husband had given her brother. But after almost killing the guy, Cooper supposed it was fitting. Guilt-easing, at least.

And at least this time he acknowledged the delay, saying he hadn't really expected Cooper to find her so quickly, after they'd been searching for months.

If it was placating flattery, it worked, Cooper thought wryly. Made him feel good, anyway.

Until he realized that it truly was almost over. Tomorrow, or two days if Jones overnighted in New York or someplace, brother and sister would be reunited, and his job would be done.

And Nell Parker would probably vanish as if she'd never existed. Because in fact, she never really had. Tanya Jones

Brown would reemerge, glamorous, rich and society page worthy, and go back to her life, all this likely forgotten after the first charity gala her husband put on.

Her husband.

He felt like he'd been punched. Which was ridiculous; it wasn't like he hadn't known. He just hadn't thought about it lately. Why should he? What did it matter to him that she was still married to some high-powered type who did fundraising for the upper crust of business and politics? A noble kind of guy, her brother had said, who had raised millions for charity over the years.

But if he was so noble, why had his wife run? Why hadn't she turned to him for solace and support when she thought her brother dead? If it had truly been an accident that night…

That was the one thing that had bothered him about this case since the beginning. But now that he'd met her, seen how wary and skittish she was, it made more sense. She was a sensitive type and probably just couldn't handle staying where it had all happened. And he certainly understood the need to simply get away—he'd surely wanted to after his father had died. She'd just carried it a little far.

But the bottom line he needed to remember right now was that she was still married to the guy. And for all his many sins he'd never swum in that pool and never intended to start.

No matter what that simple, heartfelt hug had done to him.

"So why did you leave California?"

The abrupt question caught Nell off guard. They were walking to the café today; she'd decided she'd been eating far too well lately and needed the exercise. Cooper had shown up at her door just as she was leaving, offered her a ride as usual. She was tempted, especially after yesterday's lovely expedition, but had held firm. When she'd declined he had affably agreed and decided to walk with her.

It had been pleasant, until they'd reached the waterfront

and he'd hit her with that question again. And her own sudden, harsh reaction told her just how far she'd let down her guard with this man.

Fool, she told herself.

"The heat got to me," she answered, thinking it true on many levels.

"What about your friends?"

She nearly laughed at that, but stifled it, knowing it would come out bitter and harsh. Pitiful as it sounded, she had no real friends. She'd lost touch with—or been cut off from—anyone she'd known before her marriage. New friends had all been Jeremy's. Selected and approved by him as suitable accoutrements to the lifestyle he'd built. And more importantly, all with connections that sooner or later could be of use to him.

"They haven't missed me much," she said.

"I don't believe that," he said.

"Thank you," she said, despite thinking his response had just been an automatic, polite thing to say. Maybe that was all this was, a normal attempt to make conversation. Maybe.

"What could make you leave paradise?"

Or maybe not, she thought. Was there something more than a teasing generality in his tone? Why did he keep asking about it? Suspicion bit deep.

"It's far from paradise, especially these days. I don't miss it."

"Don't miss the beach, the sun, the famous people, the parties?"

An icicle-cold chill knifed through her. She bit her lip in an effort to stay calm—and quiet. He had just described her life there to a T. As if he knew.

She clamped down on the panic that seemed to sleep only periodically, ready to awaken at full strength at any slight hint of danger. And this hadn't been just a hint. More like a sledgehammer, pounding everything she'd ever tried to put behind her back to full, terrifying life again.

She fought the urge to run, right here and now. Mainly because she couldn't decide where to run to. Into the café, where they'd finally arrived and where he was following her to anyway? Back home, where he was in essence living himself?

Pain tightened around her heart as she thought of leaving what she truly had come to think of as home. And Roger, who had been nothing short of a godsend to her, and the first real friend she'd had in years.

"I'm sure there are people who'd want you to come back," he was saying.

She nearly screamed it at him then, that yes, there was one who would want her back, so he could finish what he'd started.

"You should be in diamonds, at glittering galas, all that."

Her heart was pounding now. In a very different way than it usually did around him. He was coming too close to the truth, and there was only one reason she could see for it, one reason he would say such things about the plain, nondescript person she'd made herself into.

He knew. Knew who she was, or had been. And there was only one way that could be.

Jeremy had finally found her.

Chapter 14

Cooper stared down into his mug. Not even the Waterfront's rich brew could distract him at the moment.

He'd been worried enough that he'd come back for lunch, telling Nell he'd been out anyway to pick up some parts for *The Peacemaker*. She'd looked, oddly, more tired than she had this morning. Or worried. Maybe that was it. She'd been surprised to see him. And then warier than ever. And unlike the first time he'd come in here, he had no doubts she was very aware he was watching her.

And more suspicious than ever.

He looked over toward the kitchen, where she was in deep conversation with Riley, the ex-Navy cook. As he looked, the man reached out and put a hand on her arm, as if to steady her.

He'd really spooked her this time. And he wasn't sure why. Obviously it was his talk about her life before, but why would that spook her? Even if she suspected he wasn't being honest with her, why would she be afraid? It wasn't like he was a threat to her. In fact, once she found out why he was really here, she'd be overjoyed.

She was, he thought, an enigma. He tried to put himself in her head. A tragedy breaks her heart, she leaves to get away from it, ends up here, drawn by memories of a long-ago, happier time. Up to there, it made sense to him. The drastic changing of her looks seemed extreme, but he stuck with his conclusion that it was a female thing he'd be better off not trying to figure out.

On that thought he looked back toward the kitchen, but she must have finished her conversation with Riley because he was back to work, pulling a fresh loaf of the local bakery bread off the shelf above the grill.

He went back to his musings, trying to unravel the mystery that was Tanya Brown/Nell Parker. So after all that, she meets a stranger, they become acquainted, she does him a favor, they spend some time together and despite the edginess he can't quite explain, seem to be getting along fine. Well, minus that moment on the trail to the falls, when he'd thought she was going to run screaming into the woods as if she'd seen Sasquatch.

And then he asks a couple of simple questions anyone might ask, out of his own curiosity about why someone would leave a life many—not him, but many—would envy. He'd just been trying to gain some insight into why she seemed so wary all the time. But she freaks. Why?

It made no sense to him. She had reason to be emotional, and perhaps even touchy, but why was she afraid? And what was she afraid of?

Doubts began to assail him, doubts about many things. Was there more to this than he'd been told?

He took another sip of coffee, trying to slow his racing thoughts. The rich brew was merely warm now, and he was down to the last few swallows in the mug. Odd, Nell would usually have him topped off long before now.

He looked around, but didn't see her. And then Sheila, the woman who worked the register, came by with the pot.

"Where's Nell?" he asked.

"Something came up. She asked me to cover for her."

Cooper frowned. She must have left through the back door.

The restrooms were back there, so when he'd seen her heading toward the back, he'd assumed that was her destination. And she hadn't said anything about an errand. Not that she had to tell him her schedule, but wasn't that something you might well mention in casual conversation about the day ahead?

"She's gone? Where?"

Sheila looked at him assessingly. "You're the one staying out at Mr. Donlan's, right? On the boat?"

He nodded, not surprised word had gotten around; it seemed everybody knew everybody's business around here. Except for Nell, whom they all seemed to conspire to protect. Not that he could blame them; she inspired the same sort of feelings in him.

"Guess it's all right then," she said. "Not sure where she went. She never takes any time, so I don't mind."

"When did she leave?"

The woman glanced at the old-fashioned pendulum clock on the wall. "About twenty minutes ago."

She'd gone right after talking to Riley, then. And he'd been sitting here like a lump, lulled into complacency by her consistent routine.

"When's she coming back?" he asked.

"Not sure. She borrowed Riley's car, so I'm guessing it could be a while."

He set his mug back down sharply. *A car. Damn.*

The woman moved off to the others suffering from empty coffee cups. Cooper shifted his gaze to the man in the kitchen, whose conversation with Nell was now explained. She'd been asking for the car. An occurrence so rare it had brought on that gesture of concern.

He got up and walked over to where the man was lifting a basket of French fries out of the fryer. Riley was a direct sort of guy, so he didn't bother with niceties.

"Where'd Nell go?"

The man hooked the basket on a stand, letting the oil drain back into the fryer, never looking up. Or answering.

"Riley?"

Bread went onto the big grill, next to some bacon and a couple of burgers. Still no answer.

"Where did she go?" he asked again.

Finally the man looked at him. "Not your business."

"I'm just worried about her."

"Then leave her alone. That's what she wants."

"She took your car. So it's not anywhere close by or she'd just walk."

"Clever boy, aren't you?"

The way the man said it, it wasn't a compliment.

Sheila brought him two orders then, and he turned to his work with such intent that Cooper knew he'd get nothing more out of the man. Not that he needed it. Because he already knew, deep in his gut, with that perception his father had once been proud of.

He'd spooked her, all right. Right into running.

He tossed a five down on the counter and went out the back door, just in case he was all wrong and she was already on her way back with Riley's car, whatever errand it had been accomplished. He wasn't surprised when the single parking space to the rear was empty; he would have been surprised if she, or the car, had been there.

He swore inwardly again, harsher this time. He should never have brought up her past. There was no need. His job was only to keep her in sight. He'd been indulging his own selfish curiosity, had gone too far and now she'd rabbited on him. That he still didn't understand why didn't matter. What mattered was he had to find her again, and fast. And then he had to do whatever it took to keep her here.

He started walking, back the way they'd come this morning. She'd go home first, wouldn't she? Gather up her things? And…say goodbye to Roger? That thought made him wince; he knew she thought the world of the old man. And vice versa. How would she explain?

His thoughts stopped as if they'd hit a wall. Would she even have to explain? Or did the man who'd become her friend and protector already know why she was so scared?

He had to get there. Fast. To either find her, or get information out of Roger.

And if she is there? What are you going to do, tie her up?

He swore a third time, this time aloud and with a clenched jaw.

There was only one way to do this, and her brother was just going to have to understand that. He yanked out his phone and dialed the number. It went directly to Tristan Jones's voice mail, where the greeting had been changed to say he was on his way back from London. Cooper waited several minutes, until he got to where the walking path left the scenic waterfront and turned into a residential sidewalk, and tried again. Same result. Jones must be in the air right now, and so had the phone turned off.

The decision, it seemed, was his. But in reality, it was already made. It had to be more important to keep her from running than to preserve the surprise, however much her brother looked forward to the pleasure. His idiocy had probably cost him the last of his fee.

And the fact that that was the thing that bothered him least…bothered him.

He sent a short text explaining as best he could, shoved the phone back in his pocket and started to run.

Chapter 15

She was *not* going to cry.

"You're sure about this?"

"Sure enough that I can't take a chance."

Roger shifted his weight in the doorway of her cottage. The cottage that she'd come to love. The landlord who had become much more; a dear, trusted friend. In a life devoid of such friends for a long time, she'd found several here. And it was tearing her apart to think of leaving. So she started to pack faster.

She'd gotten a little lax in the past month or so, easing up on her determination to keep possessions at a minimum. She'd arrived here with a twenty-five-inch duffel bag, and now she had enough to fill two of them.

She'd wear the heavy jacket and her sheepskin boots; it was chilly enough. That would save her a lot of room. She would take the little native carving Roger had given her—no way she could leave that behind. And the beautiful blown glass orca she had bought on impulse with her first paycheck from the café. And of course the thick, soft and delightfully warm scarf Sheila had knitted for her last month. Nell had been stunned at the thoughtful gesture, but Sheila simply laughed and said she'd already buried her family and friends with knitted gifts, and she was delighted to have a new person to swath in miles of yarn.

Nell sighed. Sheila had promised to teach her the craft this winter, when things slowed and the café went to winter hours. She'd actually been looking forward to it. She half-suspected the woman had a herd of sheep in her backyard, keeping her in wool.

"Do you really think your husband sent him?"

"I can't take the chance. He was asking too many questions about where I was from, what my life was like."

Roger cleared his throat. "Nell, dear, he's a young man interested in a pretty, sweet young woman. Why wouldn't he ask?"

"Because I'm neither," she muttered, as she stuffed a pair of socks into a small void in the corner of the duffel.

"You've gone to great lengths to disguise it," Roger admitted, "but a discerning eye can see what's really there. And I suspect your Cooper has that."

"He's not my Cooper!"

It came out sharply, much more vehemently than the disclaimer deserved if it was the casual, meaningless retort she'd meant it to be.

"And you're sorry about that, aren't you?" Roger said softly.

She was sorry about many, many things. Not the least of which was leaving this place, this friend.

"Maybe I'll be back," she said, aware she sounded almost desperate but unable to help it. "That's probably the last thing he'd expect."

"You must do what you think is best," Roger said. "But you'll always be welcome, Nell. Know that."

She lost her battle not to cry. Roger quickly came to her, pulled her into a gentle hug. For a moment she felt like the surrogate daughter he'd once called her. His embrace was warm, comforting.

And carried none of the explosion of heat Cooper Grant's

embrace had caused in her. Which only told her how she'd been fool enough to let her guard down.

Although she had to admit, now that she was out of his presence, she was starting to wonder if maybe she'd been wrong. If perhaps Roger wasn't right, that they had been only casual, normal, curiosity-based questions.

You only can think that because right now you don't have those eyes turned on you, she told herself sternly. And she knew it was true; out from under the intensity of his gaze it would be easy to convince herself it had been innocent. She wanted to convince herself. Because she didn't want to leave.

She wondered how long she was going to be paying for the worst choice she'd ever made.

Stop it, she ordered herself. *Tris is the one who really paid for your decision. So quite whining.*

"You'll take Riley's car back? And explain for me?"

"Of course."

It was a shabby thing to do. She should talk to the man herself, on the phone at least. But she'd scrupulously avoided ever having a cell phone because of the tracking possibilities, and she didn't want to call anyone until she was safely away.

"Now I'll go gather up some food for you to take," Roger said, turning to his solution to most difficulties. "Come up to the house when you're done, then I'll take you to the bus station." He gave her a final squeeze. "I shall miss you deeply. Find your way back as soon as you can."

She hugged him back, and after he'd gone she simply stood there for a long silent moment, fighting tears once more.

"Pack," she muttered, and went back to it.

A few minutes later she was nearly ready to zip up the bag. She picked up the last piece tossed on the bed, her Waterfront Café sweatshirt, and pondered. The T-shirts she had neatly folded and stacked, ready to be returned to the café, but the sweatshirt was the only one she had. She should give it back, too, but...

She packed it, figuring her pay due from the weekend shifts, that would have been on her check this Friday, would more than cover it, plus the inconvenience of her sudden departure.

The T-shirts could go to whoever replaced her. Roger had said he'd take them back for her when he took back Riley's car, just as he'd agreed to take back the stack of library books on her nightstand. Of course, they were checked out on his card… and what would she have done without them as distraction in the long, quiet hours when the memories hovered and she was fighting the plunge into the dark chaos her life had become?

Mad, she thought. She'd have gone stark, raving mad. She would—

A sound at the door made her jerk upright. She hadn't moved fast enough. Cooper Grant stood in the doorway.

"What the hell are you doing?"

His query was sharp, short and as intense as his gaze. But she couldn't help noticing what appeared to be a touch of relief in his manner. The possible reasons for that weren't something she cared to contemplate. He was also breathing deeply; had he run here from the café? He didn't seem the type, but she wasn't surprised he was capable of it. He looked in shape to run more than two miles if he had to. Hadn't she felt his strength, just yesterday?

"Packing," she said, needlessly. "I have to…go somewhere."

"Where?"

"It's an emergency," she began, thinking that much was certainly true.

He frowned. "What's wrong?"

"None of your business."

"Nell…" he began, taking a step toward her. She backed up the same distance he moved, all the while aware he could get to her easily.

"Don't try to stop me."

As soon as the words were out she regretted them. No point in warning somebody when you had absolutely no means of following through.

Cooper ran his fingers through tousled hair. She heard a two-note message chime from his cell phone. He ignored it. He stayed focused on her.

"What the hell did I do to set you off?" he asked, sounding truly bewildered. "Just because I asked a few questions?"

"Why *did* you ask them?" she countered, quickly stuffing the small bag that held her toothbrush and the few other toiletries she had into the duffel, then zipping it up with a sharp jerk that betrayed her emotions.

"Curiosity. Interest. What's wrong with that?"

She ignored the sharp-edged comment. Kept packing. She wasn't sure she could bluff her way out of this. He was too perceptive, and her reactions had been too definite for him to be fooled. But the thin hope that he didn't know she knew was all she had.

"Where are you going?"

She almost said "I don't know," because it was the truth. She had no idea. Maybe she would have to find that boat to take her to Alaska. Too bad the one person she knew with a boat was the one who was making this necessary.

It occurred to her then that he might well follow her, or try to. And she didn't know how to deal with that. She'd managed to get this far because Jeremy hadn't expected her to have the nerve to actually leave, and because he thought so little of anything outside himself.

"I thought we were friends," he said. "At least, I thought you thought we were."

"I did." The words were out, in a pitiful near-whine, before she could stop them. And before she considered the odd way he'd phrased that.

She heard the slam of the door of the big house. Roger. Was he headed to his garden for something to harvest for her, or was he coming back here? And with a jolt that was almost physical her priorities shifted. She couldn't let him be hurt. Not for her sake. And she knew he would try to help, to protect her. He was tough, and strong, but he was still a man in his seventies. And he was the best friend she'd had in a very long time.

She'd rather die than let anything happen to him. The very idea made her throw caution—and her only advantage, that he didn't know she knew—to the winds.

"Don't you dare hurt him."

She said it through clenched teeth, with a fierceness she felt down to her bones.

Cooper looked completely taken aback. "Hurt him? Roger? Why on earth would I hurt Roger?"

"Because it would hurt me. And that's what he wants."

His demeanor changed, shifted. In an odd way it reminded her of Tris, which made no sense.

"What who wants? Who wants to hurt you?" he asked, his voice soft yet intense. And demanding an answer.

She had to end this now, she couldn't risk Roger being hurt. She couldn't carry any more guilt.

"You know damned well. Didn't he tell you why I left? His version, anyway?"

Cooper blinked. He looked genuinely puzzled. "Whose version?"

No denial that she'd left for a reason, she noticed. And she was more certain than ever that she was right. She ignored the pain that was trying to well up inside her with the ease of long practice. She focused on the immediacy of the moment, and what she was going to do. Was he going to try and stop her? Physically? That was the thought that was paramount in her mind as she tugged free the shoulder strap of the duffel.

She didn't think he was armed. She'd never seen any sign of a gun, although she was far from an expert and supposed he could have a small one hidden somewhere. Of course, guns weren't the only possibility. She swallowed tightly, remembering the night Jeremy had threatened to carve her into pieces; did Cooper carry a knife?

"The man who hired you," she said bluntly.

"Nell," he began, but she barely heard. She was looking at his face, and saw only one thing; the uncomfortable truth.

The last tiny hope she'd held crumbled inside her. And for the first time she wondered exactly what orders Jeremy had given him.

And for the first time, she didn't really care. Something bigger had died inside her, and it made her voice flat, dull, when she spoke.

"Did he tell you to kill me, or bring me back so he could?"

Chapter 16

Cooper Grant was rarely shocked. Surprised, startled, occasionally stunned, but not shocked. But she had done it.

Kill her?

He knew he was gaping at her, speechless.

"You didn't think I'd guess? I almost didn't. You're good, don't worry. You had me fooled."

He gave a shake of his head. "Nell," he said again.

"No need for pretense now. You can use my real name."

He wasn't sure how she'd guessed, or if her paranoia—for he was beginning to think it must be just that—had made her suspect him, but the fact was clear she was certain he wasn't who he said he was. And he supposed it didn't matter how confused she was about the rest. Because she was right.

Guilt stabbed at him, hot and sharp. And no amount of telling himself it was his job, just a job, seemed to ease the slicing pain. But right now he had to deal with the obvious fact that she was near panic, and determined to run. And there was only one way to stop her, no matter how much it might tick off the man who'd hired him.

"Listen to me, Nell—Tanya," he corrected himself. She didn't even react, which told him how certain she was that she'd been right.

Well, she had been, hadn't she?

He ignored the jabbing thought and went on. "I wasn't supposed to tell you. He wanted the pleasure himself."

"Oh, I'm sure he did."

Her voice was so harsh, so bitter, it scraped at him like a claw. He had to fight through the sensation to clear his thoughts; her anger at him was one thing, he'd expected that to some extent—people didn't like being fooled—but this was something else.

Think, idiot, he ordered himself. She still thought her brother was dead. So what the hell was going on?

He decided the best thing to do, before she got it in her head to bolt and he had to physically stop her, was to just get it over with.

"Tristan's alive."

There, it was out. But the words just hung there, in dead air. She didn't even blink.

"Is that what he told you to tell me? That my brother was alive?"

"It was your brother who hired me," he said.

A deep, awful sort of agony flickered across her face, settled in her eyes as she stared at him.

"My God," she breathed. "How could somebody so cold and cruel come across as so—" She stopped short, let out a clipped, utterly bitter laugh that clawed at him even harder. "Never mind. Obviously the problem is with me. I was too stupid to see through either of you."

Cooper was beginning to feel in over his head. He hated this, hated that she could look at him like that, talk to him with that tone in her voice. But he had to think, and clearly. She was so convinced Tristan was dead, of course she thought anyone who'd tell him he wasn't was cold and cruel. And there was only one person he could think of who could be the other one she was referring to.

But none of that mattered right this moment. What mattered was putting an end to this torture. Now.

even if she did, would she have hidden her reaction behind a facade of cool, worldly experience?

He made himself focus on the moment, on getting her through this. This, at least, he was here for. And if his own tangled emotions were anything to go by, she must be in internal chaos.

She shifted, looked up at him. "Who are you?"

The question took him aback for an instant; of all the things she could ask, she chose that? He quashed the spark of pleasure he felt, that he was the first thing, telling himself it had nothing to do with he himself and everything to do with the fact that he was the safest topic for a mind that had to be spinning.

"Besides a liar, I mean," she added.

Ouch.

"Everything I've told you is the truth," he said.

"It's just all based on one, huge lie."

"It just wasn't all of the truth."

She was looking at him as if he'd utterly betrayed her. The pain in her eyes, jabbed at him. He didn't understand—she should be so happy her brother was alive that nothing else mattered. And he didn't know whether to be flattered or worried that apparently he mattered.

"And it wasn't my idea," he said, a note of urgency in his voice as the explanation tumbled out. "It was Tristan's. He wanted you to see him in the flesh. He said you wouldn't believe it otherwise. He ordered me not to tell you."

"But you did."

He gestured at the bag. "You were going to run."

"I had no choice."

Her voice was flat, almost lifeless. Somehow none of this was happening as he'd expected.

"But you do, now," he said, trying to sound encouraging. He had no idea why she'd felt so desperate, but everything had changed for her now.

"What are you? A private investigator or something?"

"Of sorts," he admitted.

"A PI who lives on a boat? Read a lot of mysteries?"

"Who I am doesn't matter."

"It does to me. If you'd lie about who you are, what else would you lie about?"

She had a point, and he didn't think a discussion about lies of omission would be helpful right now. He tried to organize his words, wishing he hadn't had to prepare them literally on the run.

"Nell, listen to me. Your brother was badly hurt that night, but he survived. He's been looking for you ever since. He's ecstatic that you're okay. I just got a message that he's on his way here. He'd be here already, but he was in London when I found you here."

There. That should do it, he thought.

She'd gone very still during his outburst of explanation. Then, slowly, slowly enough that he didn't reach to stop her, she stood up. Still, he tensed as she took one long step back, out of his reach.

"There's one person you left out of your nice little story," she said.

He didn't like the way she sounded. That bitterness was back, and it made him want to wince.

"Your husband? He's been coordinating the search down south. Tristan said he feels awful about what happened. But things like that do happen."

"Things like…what?"

"An innocent person being mistaken for a burglar."

"There was no mistake. Except for my brother's."

"Your brother? What mistake did he make?"

"Saving my life."

And he'd thought she must be confused. "Nell," he began again. "What are you talking about?"

She stared at him. Her jaw set. Then, flatly, she answered him.

"Tristan took the bullet that was meant for me."

Chapter 17

Nell chided herself mentally for, even for an instant, allowing herself to hope that it was true, that somehow it had all been some huge, horrible mistake, that Tris was indeed alive and searching for her.

It was even more foolish than allowing herself to believe Cooper Grant.

He was on his feet, too, now, and she backed away another step. She was back to plan A, and she had to be sure she could get away from him.

"Nell, I don't know what you think happened that night, but—"

"No, you don't," she snapped. "But I was *there*. I know exactly what happened."

"It was an accident. Like I said, it happens."

"There was no accident."

His frown deepened. It was beginning to register with her that he seemed genuinely puzzled.

"But he didn't know it was your brother. It was dark, and your husband thought he was a burglar. And your brother told me your husband feels terrible about shooting him."

Her breath caught. She nearly stumbled backward a step. "What?"

"And about scaring you so," Cooper added. "It was a simple, if awful, case of mistaken identity."

She didn't believe for a minute Jeremy felt truly awful about anything. But that didn't matter. Something else he'd said did. A lot.

"Wait," she said, barely able to take in enough breath to speak. "Are you saying Jeremy *admits* he shot Tris?"

"Of course." He looked even more puzzled. "Why wouldn't he, when it was an accident?"

"It was no—"

She broke off repeating the assertion it hadn't been an accident. She needed to know more, she needed to know exactly what Jeremy's story had been.

"What," she asked slowly, "do *you* think happened that night?"

"Nell—"

"Just tell me. Please."

She said it all the while wondering if he'd tell her the truth. Then realized that he probably would, now. He had no more reason to lie to her, did he? No more reason to ingratiate himself, to be charming and affable, to even flirt with the plain little brown bird she'd become.

Finally, with a half shrug, he answered her. "Your brother said he came over to your place late to help you plan a surprise birthday party for your husband, who woke up unexpectedly, thought he heard a burglar. He got a gun, there was a scuffle, it went off. Understandable, really. Awakened abruptly by a strange noise in the dark, a moving shadow and a gun. Not a great combination in inexperienced hands."

She took in a deep breath, trying to steady herself. "That's the…official story?"

"Yeah. For once the news reports were fairly accurate. Except for the obvious, that they assumed your brother was going to die."

He gave her a look that she guessed was supposed to be comforting. Once, just hours ago, she would have welcomed it.

"It isn't your fault, Nell. Under the circumstances, anybody would have assumed he was dead or dying. And he nearly did, but the medics brought him back and got him to the hospital in time. Barely."

"You think I didn't check? He had no pulse. He wasn't breathing." She heard her voice start to rise and stopped, fearing she was on the edge of hysteria.

"But you're not a doctor, or a paramedic, Nell. Sometimes it can seem like somebody's gone, or maybe they even are, but they bring them back. You know it happens, all the time. Believe it."

She could hear her own pulse in her ears. Was it truly possible? Could her beloved big brother still be alive?

The idea was too huge, too stunning, for her reeling mind to deal with. So instead she seized on the one thing that had jumped out at her, the anomaly that made her question all of her assumptions.

"What I can't believe is that Jeremy admitted he shot him."

Cooper's brow furrowed yet again. He looked so honestly puzzled. But then, she already knew what a good liar he was.

"Even if it hadn't been an accident, he had to, didn't he? I mean, the police would have known anyway, he had gunshot residue on his hand and sleeve."

She blinked. "They actually tested him?"

"After he admitted it anyway? Yeah. They're pretty thorough."

She wondered if they would have if he hadn't admitted firing the weapon. She couldn't help doubting it, Jeremy being who he was, and being able to talk his way into or out of anything. She'd seen it too often, seen the way he could explain away anything, could charm—

"Why would you think he wouldn't admit it?"

The question, asked in that same, genuine-sounding puzzlement, yanked her out of the fetid pool of memories.

"I thought he'd put it on me," she answered. "I thought he'd say I did it."

"You thought he'd tell the cops you shot your own brother?"

Now he sounded astonished, she thought. "That's what I expected him to do. It's one of the reasons I ran."

A long, silent moment passed before Cooper said quietly, "I think you'd better tell me your version of that night."

"The truth, you mean."

"Your truth, yes."

"*My* truth?"

He sighed audibly. "Everybody brings their own filter. To everything. That's why any cop will tell you eyewitness testimony is unreliable. Five different wits, five different versions."

"Is that what your father told you? Or was that even true, that he was a cop?"

He winced. "I meant what I said. Everything I told you was true. And yes, he said that many times. So what happened, from your point of view?"

Somehow that sounded better. Still she hesitated. Why should she trust him, after the way he'd played her?

Yeah, and who fell into his hands like a ripe apple? she thought.

He seemed willing to listen. But she knew from long, hard experience what it was like to batter herself against the undentable façade of Jeremy Brown.

"You've met Jeremy?" she asked. "Or at least, talked to him?"

"No," he said. "Just your brother."

With one of the biggest efforts of her life she put aside those words for later. And focused on the small hope engendered by the fact that Jeremy needed face time to work the major part of his twisted magic. So maybe she had a chance.

Still she hesitated. If he'd said another word, if he'd tried coaxing or prodding her, she probably would have shut down. But he didn't, he simply waited. As if he'd sensed she would tell him if he just backed off.

"Tris came over that night, all right." Her throat tightened and the next words came hard. "Because I asked him to. He was always there for me when I needed him. And I needed him that night."

She fought the shiver that gripped her, that always gripped her when she thought of that night. She'd only told this story once, to Roger, and only then because she felt he deserved to know the truth if he was going to let her stay here.

She gulped in a breath and started again, determined to get it out this time. "I called my brother not for any birthday planning—what a typical Jeremy lie—but because I knew I'd need help. I'd already told my husband I was filing for divorce. He was…*furious* isn't strong enough. Nobody, but *nobody,* leaves Jeremy Brown if he doesn't want them to. He'd made that brutally clear to me."

His eyes narrowed. "Are you saying…he was abusive?"

"Not physically. He never…hit me. Jeremy would never get his hands so dirty, or risk bruises I could show someone. He followed more time-tested methods. Isolation. Ridicule. Threats, anger, all of it. I couldn't—wouldn't—take it anymore, no matter that the entire world seemed to think he was the most charming man on the planet."

"You must have thought it, once."

She held his gaze levelly. "I did. I thought he was going to be my safe harbor. He was strong, powerful, everything I thought I needed. I was a fool." Pain jabbed at her anew. "Tris used to say I'd been fooled, and that was different. I didn't see the distinction."

"Go on," he said, leaning now against the doorjamb of

her bedroom, his arms folded casually, as if he had all day to listen. As if that phone had never rung.

As if he would give her that whole day, if she wanted it.

She shook off the silliness, steeled herself and went on; she'd started now, might as well finish it.

"For a couple of years, everything was fine. It was a new world to me, his world, and fascinating. He was doing good work, important work, I thought. And that much was true."

"Your brother told me he's raised millions for charities around the world."

If he hadn't said it so neutrally, she might have given up right then.

"He has. But gradually I began to see that he was doing it for all the wrong reasons. Power. Prestige. That he really couldn't care less about those he was supposedly helping. What he wanted was the adulation, the admiration. He craves it. Needs it to live. Needs people to think he's nearly a saint, when all the while he despises the ones he's supposedly championing. The great unwashed, he calls them."

"Arrogant."

"Very," she said. But she said it warily, not sure if he'd been voicing an opinion on Jeremy, or simply that way of thinking in general. She caught herself pacing again, almost frantically. She probably looked and sounded like a crazy woman. And wondered if he was believing any of it.

"So…that night?"

She stopped midpace. God, he'd only wanted to know what happened that night, not her entire, miserable life history. Why had she launched into all this? Why hadn't she just given him a factual report of what had happened that night? Surely she wasn't falling victim to some insane urge to make him understand, to believe in her, that she'd had no other choice, that she wasn't the villain in this piece, that her charming, charismatic, fraud of a husband was?

But she had to make him believe. Because otherwise he'd likely try and drag her back. She'd managed to get past him, to put herself between him and the door, so she could get away if she had to, but she had a feeling he had let that happen. Maybe he thought she wouldn't leave without her stuff. Little did he know how meaningless most of it was to her. She'd learned that the hard way.

She clamped down on her thoughts before they spiraled downward any further. "I'd already filed. I knew I had to." Her mouth twisted involuntarily, and she fought to go on. "Any step out of line or inappropriate word spoken required atonement in his world. And filing for divorce certainly fell into that category."

"And running away?"

"I hoped it might be better."

He blinked. "What?"

"At first I wondered if I might have accidentally done the perfect thing. That he might take advantage. Vanished wife, big mystery, lots of attention, all that. All the kind of attention he'd love."

"But…?"

She grimaced. "I'd forgotten his ultimate ambition."

"Ultimate?"

"He wants to run for office. Fitting, really. He has a politician's soul. Or is that an oxymoron?"

One corner of his mouth quirked upward at her rhetorical question. "And a vanished wife could be problematic."

She nodded.

"Your brother said you…sometimes resented all the time your husband spent fundraising. Raising money for strangers, and not spending any time at home."

She'd already known, some part of her mind had already put the pieces together in the only way they made sense. But this made her certain; there was no way Tris would ever say such a thing about her.

"That's Jeremy. Making me sound selfish, childish."

He looked doubtful. She wasn't surprised, she knew how convincing Jeremy could be. She decided to simply cut to the chase. He'd asked about that night, well, she'd tell him. And then she'd leave. For where, she still didn't know.

If he tried to stop her…well, she'd deal with that when the moment came.

"Jeremy walked in on something, all right. He walked in on Tris helping me gather some things to take. Things that were mine, mine alone," she clarified; she'd not be thought a thief on top of everything else. "Family pictures, my mother's jewelry, things Jeremy had nothing to do with."

"Nell—"

She held up a hand, and he stopped.

"I should have known better than to go back, should have gotten those things before I ever told him about the divorce. He saw what was happening. He was enraged. Violently enraged. And he had that gun. I didn't realize it immediately, but Tris did. I tried to talk to Jeremy, but he was screaming. Literally frothing at the mouth. He aimed the gun at me."

Cooper made a sound, low in his throat. She didn't look at him. She knew this was it. She would give Cooper the truth, and he would either believe her or he wouldn't.

She forced the last, ugliest part out.

"Jeremy fired just as Tris pushed me behind him."

She did look up at him then.

"It was me Jeremy wanted to kill. My brother just got in the way. It's my fault he's dead."

Chapter 18

Cooper felt a bit hammered. What his father had always told him about eyewitnesses rang in his ears. Different versions, yeah, he got that, but *this* different?

None of this made any sense, unless somebody was lying. And why on earth would Tristan Jones lie? He'd been the true victim in all this. But he wasn't sure why Nell—or Tanya— would lie, either. And she certainly hadn't seemed to be lying. He wasn't sure she was practiced enough to fake the pain and emotion that had shown in her eyes and face, and echoed in her unsteady voice.

Unless…was she really as unstable as had been inferred by her brother, and flat out stated by her husband? Had she somehow worked up this scenario in her head? Was it perhaps the only way she could accept what had happened, or what she thought had happened? Had the death—she'd thought—of her brother so traumatized her that her wounded mind had built up this false memory?

But why on earth would she think her husband had wanted to kill her? It didn't make sense. Especially if she was right about him wanting to run for office; a shooting, even an accidental one, wasn't baggage he'd want to lug into a political campaign. A divorce was nothing, compared to that. A pesky ex-wife saying bad things about you was almost de rigueur, and if he was as polished and charismatic as Nell said he was....

He shook his head sharply. He didn't know what to believe. And until her brother got here, he guessed it didn't really matter, that there was more to this whole story. More than just an already unstable woman driven over the edge by grief.

Whatever it was, once Jones arrived, once she saw he was alive, it would all sort itself out.

Unless she was telling the truth.

She was just standing there, watching him, waiting for some kind of reaction. And he didn't know what to say. Some soothing platitude designed to keep her calm would probably accomplish nothing but to set her off again. If he said he believed her, he doubted she would believe him, she was so skittish. But if he said he didn't, she'd run. And then he'd have to stop her. Probably physically. Not something he wanted to contemplate. There were other physical things he'd be more interested in—

Shit.

He groaned inwardly. This was so not what he needed. Things were tangled up enough already, with all this he-said-she-said crap rolling around. The last thing he needed was to get emotionally involved in this mess. Yet he couldn't deny the growing unease, fear and urge to stand between her and whatever was coming.

He shook his head in reply. At worst, she was mentally troubled. At best, she was...

Telling the truth?

And there he was again. What if she was telling the truth?

"Just...hang on a second, all right?"

He pulled out his cell, checked the text message queue. The last two were from Jones, the first telling him he'd arrived, and was renting a car, the second that he was now aboard the Washington State ferry and would be at the address Cooper had given him in less than an hour.

And that had been an hour ago. In the middle of hearing her version of that night's bloody events.

If she was lying, or confused, because of her brother's death, things were going to be fine momentarily.

If she was telling the truth, things were about to get very ugly. Because if she was telling the truth, that meant he'd been lied to. In a particularly nasty way, for a particularly nasty reason.

"Nell, listen to me—"

"Why?" She grabbed up her duffel bag by the long strap and slung it over her shoulder. "You've lied to me from day one."

He started to protest, then gave up on arguing the finer points of lies of commission and omission. It didn't really matter now. What mattered was her brother was going to arrive here any second.

Or someone was.

His mind was racing. He was facing two diametrically opposed possibilities. Her brother was right, and she was borderline unstable and thus her version was untrustworthy. This version held more weight, logically, because he'd read the news story, spoken to the man, who sounded eminently reasonable. But he also knew there was a tendency to believe what you'd heard first.

Second, she was telling the truth. Which meant she'd been caught up in a horrible situation, had managed to escape it, and he had brought disaster down on her. Not to mention that if she was telling the truth, he wasn't sure anymore of anything.

Including who had hired him.

The sound of a car door slamming from outside told him the moment had arrived. Her expression, a painful mix of fear and hope made him realize she, too, was caught between two possibilities, at least as far as her brother was concerned. Her knuckles were white where her fingers were wrapped around the strap of her bag.

"Nell—"

"You bastard," she hissed.

He stopped breathing. She wasn't looking at him, she was looking through the cottage's front window. But there was no doubt the epithet was meant for him. He looked, saw a man approaching. Wearing a black wool coat over a suit that also looked expensive and custom-tailored. And walking like a man who felt he owned everything within his sight.

Charm, charisma and power.

He'd been had.

"Damn you." Nell's voice was low and harsh, and it bit deep. "You knew all along, didn't you? You just strung me along, used my brother—my dead brother!—to keep me here. You knew he was really dead but you lied to me, let me hope—"

"I didn't know," he protested, feeling more than a little sick. "I never—"

She didn't wait for whatever lame explanation he might have been able to come up with. She turned on her heel and darted toward the back of the cottage. There wasn't a back door, but there was a large window that looked down toward the water. There was a narrow sidelight with old-fashioned louvers on each side, and that was where she stopped, grabbing at the narrow strips of glass, pulling them out, making an opening. There wasn't time, but that didn't stop her from trying, and she almost made it.

And then the man in the suit was there, clearly following Cooper's helpful, detailed directions exactly. He didn't even acknowledge Cooper; he was utterly focused on the woman who turned to face him. She'd already tossed her bag through the gap, but she hadn't had time to get through herself. She held that last glass louver in her hand, and Cooper had the feeling she was assessing its usefulness as a weapon.

"Leaving so soon, my dear?"

The man walked toward her. Cooper moved that way, too, now; the smug, sarcastic tone of the man's voice erased any last doubts. While this was indeed the man he'd talked to on the phone, any trace of the loving brother he'd professed to be had vanished. And it suddenly became clear why the man had been so careful to communicate only by text messages or email since Cooper had found Nell. Or Tanya. He'd been afraid she might hear and recognize his voice at some point.

"And my, don't you look...rustic," he said.

"Go to hell," she said.

Cooper reached her just as the man shook his head and made an exaggerated sound of disapproval. "Really, such language. So common. But then, you always were, under the polish I gave you. But it's a habit you'll have to break, once we get home."

"I'm not going anywhere with you, you lying murderer."

"Easy, Nell," Cooper said softly, as he reached her side and turned to face the newcomer. He hoped she would understand he meant he was on her side, literally and figuratively, but instead she shot him a sideways glance that repeated the *Go to hell,* as clearly as if she'd said it to him, too.

"You are coming with me. You will come back home, be the loving, repentant wife you should be."

"I filed for divorce."

He waved a hand. "Oh, that. Silly of you, my dear. That paperwork was destroyed long ago. We're going home, and I will publicly forgive you for the anguish you've put me through, and see that you get the help you need for your mental condition. I only want to take care of you, dear."

"How noble of you." Nell's voice was nothing less than a jeer.

"Exactly. And it will be seen as such. The sympathy factor will be immense."

Cooper stared at the man. What Nell had told him was playing back in his mind, and the man was doing nothing to disprove her assessment of him.

"You're a fool if you think I'll go along with your scheme," she said.

"Oh, but you will. You will, or I'll be forced to confess the truth, that it was really you who shot your own brother that night, and I, as the loving, protective husband I am, was willing to sacrifice myself to save you. You were just so unstable, I feared for your life if you had to go to jail. For me, win-win."

Cooper shot a glance at Nell; he might have believed Brown's story if she hadn't already predicted he'd do just that, the man was that smooth.

And he had passed a lie detector test. And while they weren't infallible, they were a heck of a tool. Was Brown good enough to defeat one? Maybe. He sure as hell had fooled him.

"That's enough," Cooper said.

The man flicked a glance at him, as if he'd forgotten Cooper was even in the room. He shrugged off his earlier words.

"Oh, that's just my impatience talking." He smiled then, a powerful, charming smile Cooper imagined got him many things. "And I apologize, I've been remiss. Thank you. You've done your job, more than adequately."

"You're not Tristan Jones."

The man waved a hand in an imperious gesture of dismissal. "You'll get the rest of your money, don't worry."

"You lied to me. From the beginning."

"Please," Brown said in a tone that matched the gesture. "What does it matter to you, as long as you're getting paid?"

"It matters," Cooper said grimly.

He wasn't sure exactly how much of Nell's story he believed, but it was obvious this man was a practiced and effective liar. Enough to beat a lie detector? He didn't know. And being a liar didn't necessarily make him a killer.

But that he'd lied to Cooper from the get-go put the weight of truth on Nell's side of the scale, in his book. And she'd predicted accurately his threat to blame her for her own brother's death, even if Brown brushed it off as mere impatience. Cooper had no doubts where he stood.

"She's not going anywhere until I sort this out," Cooper said.

Jeremy stiffened. "May I remind you, you work for me?"

"No," Cooper said flatly.

Brown's gaze flickered, and he got the feeling that was a word he didn't hear often. Except maybe from his wife? He nearly glanced at her then, but something about the way Brown's expression had changed kept him focused there. Plus, he was aware she had been fingering the glass piece she held with a definite intent, and he didn't want Brown noticing.

"I was hired by Tristan Jones."

Brown smirked. "Hired by a dead man?"

Cooper sensed, as if it were a physical thing, the last whisper of hope leave Nell. Her hands stilled on the glass louver. She had to have known, the minute she'd seen her soon-to-be-ex-husband, but it took those words to smother that final, stubborn flicker.

And he had done it to her. Given her that false hope.

She said nothing, but Cooper was afraid the confirmation of what she'd known all along might be enough to push her to do something foolish. Worse, he was afraid she might not care if anything happened to her.

"I was hired under false pretenses. By a liar who used the name of a dead man to perpetrate a fraud. By any code, I'm not responsible to you anymore."

"Code?" Brown sounded incredulous. "What kind of ridiculous talk is that?"

"Everyone has one they live by," Cooper said. "Even if they don't realize it. Even if it's twisted."

"Please," Brown scoffed. "Grow up. What do you think you are, some knight in shining armor, come to rescue the fair maiden? Well, she's neither fair nor a maiden, though she might as well be for all the good she is in bed."

Nell didn't even blink, and Cooper had the feeling this was hardly the first time she'd heard that assessment. It fit with what she'd told him. *Isolation. Ridicule. Threats, anger...*

"Real gentleman, aren't you?" Cooper sneered. "As far as I'm concerned, I was hired by her brother. Not you. I owe you nothing."

"I don't need anything more from you," Brown said. "We'll be leaving now."

"I don't think so. Maybe the police need to come sort this out."

Brown laughed. Nell shook her head. "It won't do any good. Trust me. He'll talk his way out of it, subtly threaten them with who he is, the people he knows, people in high places who owe him favors."

"Not all cops play that game," Cooper said.

"You believe that? Then you're as big a fool as she is," Brown said. "And I am out of patience for fools. This is over. We're going home."

He took a step toward Nell. A blast of urgency shot through Cooper. And he knew in that instant he wasn't about to let Nell go with this man, not until he had time to sort out truth from lie.

And he had the distinct feeling Brown wasn't going to like that. At all.

Chapter 19

The moment Cooper moved, Nell could almost feel Jeremy adjusting, reassessing. He stopped in his advance on her, and shifted his attention to Cooper. She'd seen him work before, knew he'd decided Cooper was the key. Or the impediment.

And Cooper was looking at him as if he were decidedly uncharmed.

Jeremy hadn't succeeded with him. Of course, he'd barely tried, but that was usually all it took for most people. Or perhaps he'd never intended to try and charm the man he'd hired, knowing that as soon as she saw him, the truth would be out. He must have thought it wouldn't matter to someone whose services he'd paid for. He hadn't taken into account, apparently, the possibility that Cooper wouldn't appreciate being lied to.

That was odd. Usually Jeremy thought things through better, carefully assessing the possible help or damage to himself. Collateral damage didn't matter, of course. Nor did the irony that Cooper himself had lied to her from the beginning.

"Now, now," Jeremy said, recovering his poise, "let's all just calm down."

"You first," Cooper said.

"Oh, I admit I lost my patience there. But she is the most

provoking woman." He looked at her then, with all his smug overconfidence firmly back in place.

"Come along, Tanya."

"Nell. I'm Nell, now."

If there was a more ridiculous response she couldn't imagine it, yet it had been the first thing that had sprung to her lips.

Jeremy sighed. "That's even worse than Tanya. I loathe alliteration among siblings."

"You loathe everything and everyone except yourself," she retorted.

"Thank you for that brilliant analysis," he snapped, sarcasm fairly dripping from every syllable. Apparently the return of confidence hadn't been as complete as she thought; a confident man didn't snipe at others.

"If I'm so stupid, why do you want me back?"

"Precisely because you are stupid and should do as you're told. And you will. I won't have you destroying all my plans."

"You don't need me."

"But I do. It's the picture that's important, the impression. And you're already in place, and I haven't time to devote to long explanations. So you will come back and behave."

"I will not."

He ignored her. "That ridiculous haircut will have to go, and you'll go back to blonde, of course, but once you're back in appropriate clothes—and rid of those hideous glasses—you'll be presentable again."

"An accessory. That's all I ever was, isn't it?"

"What else could you possibly be? Why do you think I selected you? Because you were moldable. You'll be the perfect political wife, with a little schooling and practice."

"Aren't you afraid I'll tell the truth?"

"With your history, all it will do is remind people of my kindness and love for putting up with your mental instability. So you *will* behave."

Cooper had said nothing during this exchange, just inched

ever closer to her. Too scared to trust anyone, she edged closer to the window. She could do it, she thought, get through that space now, all she needed was a chance.

"Aren't you afraid I'll say something stupid and embarrass you?" she asked.

Jeremy nearly sneered. "No. Because you will say nothing—*nothing*—unscripted by me, ever."

"Going to buy me a teleprompter?"

His hand came up. For a moment she thought he would strike her. He'd never resorted to actual physical violence before, but perhaps he was losing his grip. And if that was true, perhaps she could use that. She had to get away from Jeremy first, then she'd decide what to do from there.

She hurled the piece of glass at his head.

Jeremy ducked instinctively. In that instant she dived through the opening that last louver had given her. Tumbled into the flower bed outside, half on her duffel bag. Scrambled to her feet. Since it was there, she grabbed the bag. And ran.

She heard Jeremy's shout. She kept running. She raced up to the driveway, to where she'd parked Riley's car. Groaned when she saw a silver sedan with a rental agency sticker blocking her in, along with Roger's car in the garage.

Roger. She had to get out of here before he came looking for her, and walked into the nightmare she'd brought here.

Cooper's motorcycle was there, and it could get out along one side, but she knew nothing about controlling one, and she doubted it was something you could learn on the fly.

She'd have to run, literally. She would—

Her breath caught in her throat as she heard the front door of the big house open. Roger must have seen her. She turned to call out to him, to tell him to stay inside.

And then her new nightmare began in earnest as two things happened simultaneously.

Roger stepped out onto the porch.

And a hand came down on her shoulder from behind.

Chapter 20

"Take your hand off her."

Cooper didn't look at Roger, who was looking down at him from the front porch of his house. He kept his eyes—and that hand—on Nell, who had whirled on him.

"Let go of me," she demanded, trying to twist away from him.

"Not until you slow down and listen."

"Slow down?" She stared at him incredulously. "With *him* likely to show up any second?"

She yanked her arm, but he held on. He couldn't let her vanish again, not until he had the whole story, and not until he knew she was safe. He didn't think he'd ever had a situation do a one-eighty so fast in his life, and he wanted the truth. All of it.

"Cooper Grant, you let go of her."

The man came down the steps. For all his years, Cooper had the feeling Roger might actually be a more formidable opponent than the much younger Jeremy Brown. He was wiry, tough; and Brown, for all his sleek style, was soft.

"It's all right, Roger," he said, holding up his free hand to stop the man from whatever he was thinking of doing. But he still never took his eyes from Nell. "It won't be seconds. We've got a few minutes."

"You've deceived her—and me—since you arrived," Roger reminded him.

"There was a good reason," he told the man.

"A few minutes?" Nell asked.

"I tied him up with one of the T-shirts you left."

He didn't mention the struggle, or the restraint it had taken on his part not to beat the man bloody. He truly hated being lied to. And he wasn't having any luck convincing himself that being lied to was the reason he had wanted to do even more damage to the man who had hurt her.

"But it won't take him long to get loose," he said. "We should call the sheriff."

"No!" Her exclamation was sharp and immediate. "It will take too long, and trust me, they will never believe me, not against Jeremy. No one ever does. Let me go," she said, trying to pull free a third time. "I have to get out of here before he gets loose."

"All right," Cooper said, with the sound of a man making a quick decision. She looked startled, but stopped trying to break away. "But by the time we get this car—" he indicated the vehicle Brown had left, no doubt intentionally, sideways across the driveway "—out of here, he'll be here."

"Then what—"

"*The Peacemaker*. We'll take *The Peacemaker*. It'll be harder for him to track you over water. And he may not even have noticed it. He was pretty zeroed in on you."

"You want me to trust you, to get on a boat alone with you?"

"I want you not to be alone and on the run again," Cooper said.

Somehow he'd found the right words. He saw in the expression on her face the remnants of the fear and aloneness she must have felt as she made her escape that ugly night.

"It will give you time to think, Nell. We can figure out what to do."

Still she hesitated.

"We don't have much time," he reminded her. "It'll take a minute or two to cast off."

She glanced at Roger. The older man's gaze had never left him, but now he shifted to Nell. After a brief, silent moment, she nodded.

"I think it's all right, Roger. He helped me in there. He stood by me."

"He did tie him up. I suppose that's worth something."

"Thanks," Cooper said. He reached for her duffel. And after a moment, she let him take it. "We've got to get underway, fast." He glanced at Roger. "He may come looking for you, asking questions. He'll be the one with the swollen lip."

Roger lifted a brow at him. "Well, well. More to you than meets the eye."

"Or less to him," Cooper said. That earned him a smile from Roger, and a quick, pleased intake of breath from Nell. He'd take both.

"I'll deal with Mr. Brown," Roger said; obviously he'd been right, Cooper thought, when he'd guessed that Nell would have told him everything. She would never take the chance of bringing something like this down on the old man without warning. "I can play deaf and senile old man if I need to."

Cooper flashed a grin at him. "I'll bet you can."

"But in the meantime, I'll move that—" he pointed at Cooper's motorcycle "—into the garage. He had to notice it, since he parked next to it. So I'll tell him you two took off on it. 'Damned *smelly* thing, it went thattaway,'" he quoted in a perfect imitation of a querulous old man.

Cooper's grin widened. "Roger, it's a pleasure to know you."

"Don't you make me regret knowing you," Roger said sternly.

A noise came from below, the direction of the little cottage that had been Nell's home, followed by a string of shouted curses audible even here on the other side of the big house. Cooper saw the fear that flashed in Nell's eyes, saw the utter conviction that running was the only answer. And he discarded his own reservations, his own instincts to turn this all over to law enforcement and went with the needs of the woman who had somehow become the center of his world. And right now, she needed to get away. He wouldn't betray her again, and that's what it would feel like to her. She was too frightened, and that tore at him in a way nothing every had.

They'd figured the rest out later, when she felt safe.

Nell gave the man a swift but fierce hug. Cooper went to look through the concealing branches of the big cedar at the corner of the house. He saw Jeremy stumbling up toward the patio, one hand pressed to his split lip as if it were a mortal wound.

"Around the back of the greenhouse," he said to Nell.

She nodded.

And then they were running, toward the dock and *The Peacemaker.* She did exactly as instructed, untying the lines while he jumped aboard, ran up the steps to the pilothouse, started the engine. Then she scrambled aboard and hauled in the lines. Tidiness would come later, when they were safely away.

As would a whole lot of talking.

But for now, *The Peacemaker* was free and moving. The rest could wait.

She didn't know much about boats, other than the idea of such freedom appealed, so she had to assume piloting *The Peacemaker* really took as much concentration and focus as Cooper was giving it. Although he did it easily, hands steady on the big, old-fashioned wooden wheel she was sure was called something else in nautical jargon. He didn't seem tense or hyperalert, just competent and at ease as he guided them up the inlet that would open into a larger bay, and then out into Puget Sound proper. After that, she had no idea.

Once they'd cleared the inlet and moved into the more open area of the main bay, the wind picked up. She was thankful they were inside; she'd not been able to grab her heavy jacket, and while it wasn't cold out, it was cooler on the water, and the breeze of their passage made it seem even cooler. She was chilled even in here.

"There's a couple of spare jackets in the locker behind you," he said.

She stared at him as he stood at the wheel. She supposed that perceptiveness stood him in good stead in his line of work. Although she realized she still didn't know exactly what his work was; he'd only answered "Sort of" when she'd asked if he was a private investigator.

She got the jacket from the locker, although it took her a moment to figure out the latch. She felt better with the warm fleece on, but still she paced whenever she forgot to stop herself. She was afraid it would irritate him, but she was so wound up…

She tried harder to make herself stop the pacing. She glanced at him. He didn't seem bothered by her restlessness. Maybe he really was just giving her time and space to think. Lord knows she needed it. And he probably knew it.

There was another chair beside the wheel. She contemplated going and sitting beside him, but didn't think she could settle. She wondered if that was where his mother had sat while his father steered, as he was doing. For the first time she thought about what memories must be tied up in this boat for him.

"There's some M&M's in the galley." He spoke for the first time in a while, with a gesture toward the three or so steps that curved downward into the main cabin.

"I'm not hungry."

"I figured. But the crash is going to be ugly, and fuel now will help."

"Crash?"

"Adrenaline. Great while it lasts, but you're pretty depleted afterward."

"Oh." She gave him a sideways look. "M&M's?"

He shrugged, one side of his mouth quirking upward. "A weakness."

"Any particular color?" she asked, relieved at the almost normal conversation.

"I'm not picky." The quirk became a grin. That killer, disarming grin that seemed so real to her compared to Jeremy's practiced—literally, she'd caught him practicing it in the mirror more than once—expression. "As long as you eat them right."

"There's a wrong way?"

"Sure. Some people just grab a handful and crunch them. Way wrong."

Distracted, she asked, "And the right way?"

"One at a time. With your teeth first. Break the shell off, then go for the heart."

Kind of like you did with me?

The thought coalesced in her mind with shocking suddenness, as if it had been percolating for a long time.

It was a job for him. You were a job. Nothing more, she told herself firmly.

But if that were true, why were they here, escaping? Why was he helping her at all, when the man he'd left tied up on her cottage floor had been the one paying him?

The restlessness seized her again, coupled with curiosity, and she couldn't resist going down those steps for a look. What she saw amazed her. It was amazingly spacious, she thought. And surprisingly homey. It felt warm.

And safe.

She noticed a few details: there was a lot of polished wood in the cabin, and the upholstery had a muted blend of blue and green she liked. The plank floor in the main living area was covered with a rug, carefully cut to follow the contours of the edges of the lockers beneath the seats and the curved support mast at the center of the boat. She guessed it would be nicer on bare feet, especially on a cold morning, than the exposed wood would be.

She found the familiar brown bag on the counter in the galley. The galley itself was as amazing as the rest. There was very normal-looking sink, a small but new-looking microwave, and a refrigerator that appeared almost as large as the one in the cottage. There was even a dishwasher. And a trash compactor, which made sense when she thought about being at sea for long periods. The whole setup reminded her of some of the nicer, bigger RVs she'd seen, and she supposed the principle was the same.

She snagged up the bag and took it back up to the pilot house. Cooper took a couple of the hard-shelled candies and proceeded to eat them exactly as described. She still wasn't at all hungry but, afraid he was right about the crash, she did the same.

"Roger's a tough old bird when he has to be, isn't he?" Cooper said after a while.

She smiled despite her roiled emotions. "Yes, he is. He's remarkable." Then after a moment she asked, "Did Jeremy… fight you?"

Cooper scoffed. "Soft city boy," he said. "Never took a real punch in his life before."

"I'm sorry I missed that," she said, meaning it.

That grin again. "He went down like a sack of rice. I've hooked salmon who fought harder than he did."

She laughed. And then her breath caught at the shock of it; how could she be laughing in the middle of this?

Cooper turned to look at her, full on, for the first time. Something about his expression made her tension ease up a bit.

"That's my girl," he said softly.

The explosion of warmth inside her finished what that look had started. Her tension drained away, and she knew it had little to do with the fact that they were in wider waters now, for the moment safe from pursuit, and everything to do with the man beside her.

She stood watching him as much as the view around them as they motored on in silence for a while, or at least as much silence as was possible on a boat powered by the huge—at least to her—motor she'd seen him working on. Apparently the work had gone well, because to her albeit untrained ear, it sounded as smooth as silk. And really, it was amazingly quiet, more of a background hum than true noise.

And then they cleared the mouth of the bay, and she felt a slight twinge as land receded behind them.

She didn't think she'd shown it, but Cooper again proved his perceptiveness, and she had the stray thought that it was no wonder he was a detective, the way he could read her.

"It's okay. She's more than seaworthy, and we're not really at sea."

"Seems like it's close enough," she said, looking at the nearest land ahead, miles away. It was better, she supposed, than the open sea, with nothing ahead but the curve of the earth.

"Don't get me wrong," he said. "The sound is wide and deep and very, very cold, in its own way deserving of as much respect and caution as blue water."

"Blue water?"

"Open sea. Middle of nowhere, days or weeks away from land kind of water."

She suppressed a shudder that intensified as the swells picked up farther out and she had to put a hand on the dashboard—if that was what it was called—to steady herself. "You've done that?"

"Once or twice. Wouldn't do it for long in a stinkpot, though."

She blinked. "Stinkpot?"

"Power boat. Relying on one source of power to cross thousands of miles of ocean? Always tied to ports with fuel available? No, thanks. Give me power and sail for that."

"Oh. That makes sense."

"If blue-water sailing ever does," he said, unleashing the grin again. "Me, I'm mostly a coast-hugger these days."

She smiled. Coast-hugger.

Her breath stopped.

Trout-hugger.

The memory of how he'd used that old nickname to fool her rose up like some sort of leviathan from the deep. Wariness bit anew; this man had fooled her so thoroughly, had allayed her early—and obviously well-founded—suspicions.

Almost involuntarily she backed away from him a step. For all the good it would do. She was trapped, nowhere to go. Overboard wasn't an option, they were too far out now, and she'd heard all the stories about the short survival time in the cold of Puget Sound without protective gear.

And she wondered if, instead of escaping, she'd instead gotten herself into deeper trouble. Deeper water.

Enemy waters?

She didn't know.

And once again she was afraid her ignorance was going to cost her.

Chapter 21

He'd been watching the water around them as carefully as a driver in heavy traffic on a freeway, but now Cooper gave her a sideways, curious glance. She wasn't sure what was showing in her face, but obviously it was enough to tell him something was wrong.

"Decided you don't trust me again?"

She backed up another step this time, more hastily. "How *do* you do that? Are you a mind reader?"

"Body language. Facial expressions." And then, with another quirk of his mouth, he added, "And you're not a very good liar."

"Unlike you."

He looked back to the water. As far as she could see there wasn't another boat anywhere close, but she supposed there were other things you had to watch out for; she'd seen debris, sometimes even big logs, floating out in the sound often enough. She also noticed that there was land closer now, that they'd turned away from the wider reaches of the sound and into a narrower channel.

"Tool of the trade," he said at last. "Most times it doesn't bother me."

Most times? But it was bothering him this time? Was she supposed to believe that, that she was a special case to him?

She didn't want to delve into that, not now. There lay foolishness of the worst kind. What she needed now was answers. Honest ones.

"You said you were a private investigator 'of sorts.' What does that mean?"

"It means I do this kind of work when it comes along. But I don't go looking for it, I don't advertise and I don't have an office or a phone listing."

He answered without hesitation, not thinking about what to tell her first. Did that mean it was the truth? She hoped so.

"Then how do people find out about you? Or find you?"

"Word of mouth, from people I've done jobs for. And cops talk to cops, who talk to cops, so a lot comes my way from that."

"They send people to you?"

He nodded.

"Even if they don't know you themselves?"

The nod again. Then, as if he thought it require more explanation, he spoke again. "Some knew my father. Or knew of him. And for a lot of them, the simple fact that I'm the son of a cop killed in the line is enough for them to trust me."

Was there a jab in there for her? "So I'm supposed to trust you, too, despite the lies, because of that?"

He let the accusation of lying go by this time. When he looked at her then, his gaze wasn't casual in the least. It was intense and penetrating.

"I trusted you," he said.

She blinked. "You trusted me?"

"I trusted your assessment enough not to do what every instinct I've got was screaming at me to do. Call the sheriff."

She hadn't thought of it that way, but she had to admit he had a point. He had essentially taken her word that involving law enforcement wouldn't work, not with Jeremy. That somehow he'd weasel and worm his way out of it. That he had stature enough to make any cop anywhere think twice about getting tangled up in arresting the guy for some claim by his crazy—as Jeremy would convince them—wife. If they had their own cops would know Roger, maybe. But what they had was a sheriff's deputy with too much ground to cover.

And Cooper had gotten her away, safely. He'd stood between her and Jeremy when it had come down to the crunch. He'd changed sides rather quickly, too, all things considered.

Then again, maybe not. Maybe it had happened over the last week, from the time he'd first walked into the Waterfront.

"Yes," she answered, belatedly. "Yes, you did. Thank you."

His voice was soft, gentle when he spoke again. "What set you off just now, Nell?"

He deserved that much, she thought. "Coast-hugger."

"Coast-hugger?" It took him a moment. Then she saw realization dawn on his face. "Trout-hugger," he said.

She thought she heard a touch of sadness in his tone, but it was laced with something else, something harder, edgier.

"How did you know that name?" she demanded, all the questions welling up anew.

"He told me."

She noticed he didn't elaborate on what *he* meant because it no longer mattered. Tris was dead and had been all along. Anger threatened to rise up and take control, but she told herself he hadn't known. She believed that much; he'd said so to Jeremy's face, and the man hadn't bothered to deny it.

"But he never knew about that nickname," she said.

"You're sure?"

"Tris…didn't like him. He'd never tell him. And I certainly didn't. It was private, between us."

Obviously Tris had been right all along.

"When did your brother use it?"

"Only when we were alone. When we were kids he used

to use it all the time, to tease me. When we got older, it was mostly…nostalgia, I guess. To remind us of better times."

"When your family was whole."

He said it so quietly it shouldn't have held the emotion it did. But she was suddenly, powerfully reminded that this man understood in the way only someone who'd been through it could.

"Yes," she whispered.

"When was the last time he used it? The nickname, I mean."

She didn't have to think hard for that one. "In an email. On Mom's birthday."

"So your husband could have seen it."

"No. He would have had to figure out my password and snoop into my—"

She broke off, realizing how silly that sounded under the circumstances.

"That was stupid. Of course he did."

"He wouldn't necessarily have even needed your password. There are programs for monitoring all computer activity and sending someone else a report. Like they use to track kids."

She grimaced. Kids. Jeremy treated her just like one, so why wouldn't he there, too? And elsewhere? Anger at her own blindness spiked through her.

"He probably had everything I did monitored. I was just too stupid to see it."

"Innocent doesn't translate to stupid," Cooper said, "in any language."

That harder edge was back in his voice, and this time she realized what it was.

"You're angry."

He looked at her straight on then. "Angry? No. What I am is furious."

She realized abruptly it was nothing less than the truth, realized she'd sensed it in him for some time now. Ever since those moments at Roger's when he'd realized who had really hired him.

"I was lied to," he said, confirming her guess. "And I believed it all."

And she, despite some cautions from that little voice in her head, believed him.

"If I'd seen him, talked to him in person," Cooper said, "I might have suspected. But everything was on the phone and then email or text messages."

"Or maybe not," she said, feeling the oddest urge to console him. "Jeremy is very, very good."

"He was pretty easy to read back there," Cooper said.

"That is the most…indiscreet I've ever seen him in front of anyone else." She drew in an audible breath. "He must hate me so much he let his guard down."

"Or he hates the idea that you slipped away from him. Out of his control."

Oddly, the words were comforting. It was easier to think of someone hating what you'd done than hating you yourself with that kind of fury. Because it would have to be that kind of anger to shake Jeremy's usually cool control.

"I'm sorry, Nell. Or should it be Tanya, now?"

"I don't think I'll ever feel like Tanya again," she said. "But sorry about what?"

"I believed him. And because I believed him, I didn't go beyond what he himself provided in the way of information. So I put you through hell all over again. I raised your hopes about your brother, and it was all a lie."

The words came out in such a rush she knew he had to have been thinking them for a while. As he apologized so humbly for everything that had had her so angry with him in the first place, she found it hard to hang on to that anger.

"I just kept thinking it was going to be worth it," he said. "I didn't like the idea, but he insisted. Said he wanted the pleasure of telling you himself, and that you wouldn't believe me, anyway, after that night. And I told myself that when you saw your brother, alive and well, for the first time, it would all be worth it."

She hadn't thought of it from his point of view before; she'd been too irate. And something in his voice, in the sudden tenseness of his body, told her not all of that anger was directed at Jeremy.

And suddenly the last of her own anger drained away.

"He's very convincing," she said.

"And I'm supposed to be a detective of some sort."

He hadn't known. And he'd had reason, good reason in his view—as in his employer's orders—to keep the "truth" from her.

And he'd thought he was doing something good for her. He'd honestly thought he was going to ease her pain.

She realized they'd changed direction again, that he'd been making a sweeping and gradual right turn. Starboard, she thought. Her father had explained it once, on a flight when the captain had pointed out some landmark visible out one side of the plane. Port, he'd told her, had the same number of letters as left. The memory peg had delighted her, and she knew she'd never forget which was which again.

Odd, she hadn't thought about that in years. Most of her memories of her father were tainted with his disappearance.

She looked around more carefully. Tried to picture a map in her head, but she was oriented to land, not water. Up ahead she saw an odd shape of something going across the channel.

"Where are we going?"

"Back to where we were before you were so pissed at me."

It was such an odd way to put it that she drew back a little. If she was just a job to him, why would he care?

Before she could go down that treacherous road, it hit her. They were approaching the Hood Canal floating bridge.

"We're going back to the state park?"

"The neighborhood, yes."

She eyed the bridge up ahead. "Doesn't it have to open up for boats?"

"For big ones, and barges. And the Navy. We can go under the high part on the east end."

"Why there?"

"The canal's in essence a big dead end, so hopefully he'd think we'd head for more open water. Plus, it has another advantage."

"Which is?"

"It's within running distance of Bangor."

She blinked. "The submarine base?"

He nodded. "Just stray a little too close, and whoever's following you will have to deal with the might of the U.S. Navy. That would slow even Mr. Smooth down, if he took a notion to come after us afloat."

"But…so would we."

He shrugged. "Might take some time to straighten out. But it also might be worth it to see him squirm."

There was such satisfaction in his voice at the thought of causing Jeremy problems that it warmed her to the core. And for the first time in a very, very long time, she felt as if she just might have someone on her side. Someone she could trust.

But that didn't stop her from feeling a qualm when, some time later, after an uneventful passage and a successful anchoring offshore, Cooper turned to her and spoke.

"Now. Feel like telling me the whole story?"

No, she didn't. She didn't feel like telling anyone her sad, misbegotten tale.

But she also didn't feel as if she had any choice.

Chapter 22

Cooper had sensed the moment when she'd given in and begun to trust him. It seemed the apology had done it. Not that he hadn't meant it; he had. Every last word of it. He'd been lugging around guilt about lying to her from the day he'd found her. Finding out he'd bought a bag of lies himself, and in the process destroyed the fragile peace she'd built for herself had only made it worse. He didn't know if he'd ever forgive himself for that.

He didn't know how much of a scumbag Jeremy Brown really was, but at the very least he was a liar and a control freak. And if Nell's version of what had happened that night was accurate—and since Brown had already proved himself a liar, there wasn't much doubt left—then he was much, much worse.

And he used you, he added silently. *Don't forget about that.*

And he had to admit that had ticked him off enough so that he thoroughly enjoyed cold-cocking the guy back at the cottage. He'd have done more if he hadn't been so focused on finding Nell and stopping her from doing anything foolish. Like vanishing again.

Nell was watching him, a new kind of wariness in her eyes.

She may have come with him willingly, but he knew it was because she'd felt she had little choice. She didn't trust him, not completely. Not yet, anyway. But she would. And sooner rather than later, if he had anything to say about it.

They were sitting inside the main cabin, Nell with her legs curled up under her on the main banquette. It was still nice enough they could be outside on the rear deck, but she'd shaken her head rather vehemently when he'd asked.

"I feel safer in here."

"Less visible," he'd said, understanding the need. Jeremy hadn't seen them leave, but he might have heard them and guessed, at least if he'd noticed the boat at the dock when he'd arrived. Fortunately she had been moored bow forward, so he couldn't have seen the stern with *The Peacemaker* painted on it, and she wasn't distinctive enough to pick out among the thousands of boats on the sound, unless you knew the make and model well, or spent some time studying.

"You can dump the glasses, if you want," he said now, figuring that was a neutral enough subject. "And the contacts. Assuming you don't need them to see."

She looked startled. Then relieved, perhaps at the idea of removing the contact lenses. And then, after a moment, troubled.

"But if I have to run again—"

She stopped as he shook his head. "No more, Nell. This needs to be over."

A visible shiver ran through her. "You don't understand. Jeremy isn't a household name, but he has a lot of them in his pocket. He's raised money for them. That was always his real goal, to have people in power owing him. The charity fundraising he does gets more press—he sees to that— but it's just to balance the public picture. Make him seem beneficent."

"Even powerful men aren't invincible."

She shook her head. She was trembling now.

"Nell, listen to me. He's going to go down. I'll make it my life's work if I have to."

She stared at him. "Why? Just because he lied to you?"

"That's one reason," he said, realizing as he looked at her that it truly was only one reason. And that it was far from the most important one.

She was still staring at him, as if she were trying to discern those other reasons. He didn't think she'd be able to, because they were so tangled up in his head that he couldn't sort them out himself at the moment. He just knew she'd become more important to him than anything else.

"He's too big," she said. Her fingers curled into fists as she spoke, and he realized she was trying to steady herself. He stood up.

"Come on. Let's get you settled. I'll show you where things are."

She stood as well, but wariness crept back into her eyes. "You say that like it's going to be a while."

"It might be," he said. "On board, anyway. That's the good thing, we can move easily and quickly if it seems he's figured it out and starts looking for a boat. I gather he has the resources to mount a search?"

"Jeremy is a wealthy man, yes. Enough to put on the show required to be taken into the confidence of the world he moves in. But a lot of his wealth is in that power he's collected. His connections."

"The ability to pick up the phone and call in a favor?"

She looked relieved that he'd understood. "Exactly."

"Even up here?"

"He has some large donors up here, yes."

"Just how high up the chain does this go?"

She grimaced. "He helped put the president in office."

Cooper drew back slightly at that.

"I told you he was too big."

Cooper reached out and grasped her shoulders. "Nobody's too big to go down for murder. Nobody."

She drew in a deep, shuddering breath. Cooper couldn't take the fine trembling he could still feel under his hands, as if she were chilled to the bone and beyond. He pulled her closer, wrapped his arms around her. For a moment she was taut, stiff, but then the trembling won and she sagged against him.

"It's going to end, Nell. You're not alone in this anymore."

She made a tiny, stifled sound he couldn't interpret against his chest. She felt small, fragile, as he held her. And if everything she'd said was true, she'd pulled off no small miracle to escape and stay hidden this long.

And then he'd come along and brought her old hell raining down on her again.

He realized in that moment that he believed her. Completely. It had only taken a few minutes in the presence of Jeremy Brown to give credence to everything she'd told him. He might be smooth on the outside, but he was twisted and viciously sharp on the inside.

"I'm sorry," he whispered against her hair, thinking he might never say it enough to make up for what he'd inadvertently done.

He felt her shoulders lift slightly, heard her sigh. "I believed him, too, once."

She was kinder than he would have been, he thought. "I just jumped into finding you. I never looked past that first news story he sent, beyond verifying that it was genuine. If I'd looked further, I might have found out—"

He stopped abruptly, not wanting to jab her yet again with the old pain made new.

"That Tris was really dead?" she asked, doing it for him. "I understand, Cooper. Really. I know how persuasive Jeremy can be. And he's a good actor, too. I've seen him put on performances that were amazing, cultivating people I knew he despised, or was angry with, or who didn't trust him. You had no reason not to believe him."

"It was a nice change," Cooper said. "No philandering

spouse, no drug-addicted kid lost on the streets, just a sister who'd fled thinking the worst had happened, and a chance to bring some good news to her."

She leaned back in his arms, looked up at him. Her eyes glistened but her cheeks were dry, as if she'd started to cry but managed to stop it before it spilled over. He didn't know which moved him more, the thought of her in tears, or the strength it had taken to stem the tide.

She's a delicate, flighty thing, her brother—no, Brown—had said.

He ran back through his mind all the things he'd been told, things he'd thought were coming from a loving brother. All the things about her being a bit flaky, unstable and high maintenance. How he had, on some level, assumed that was a kind assessment, because her brother loved her and would cut her some slack.

Instead, what it had been was purposeful denigration by a controlling, emotionally abusive soon-to-be-ex-husband who—

He stopped his own thoughts with a sour twist of his mouth.

"What?" she asked.

"I'm having to go back and put everything he told me into the right context."

"Context?"

"Coming from him, and not your brother."

She let out an audible breath. "I can imagine what he said about me."

Cooper shook his head. "Not that. I mean, what he said about you never did fit with what I was seeing, once I found you."

"Thank you." She sounded as if he'd done much more than simply credit what he'd seen with his own eyes over what he'd been told. And she was looking at him in a way that made his pulse kick up a notch, as if he'd done something…heroic. When all he'd done was be a fool.

"What I meant was what he said about…himself."

"Himself?" Her brow furrowed. "You mean as Tris, talking about Jeremy?"

He nodded. "He talked about what a great guy Jeremy was, how the shooting was an accident and completely understandable, how guilty he felt about it."

"Jeremy," she said flatly, "never felt guilty about anything in his life."

Cooper grimaced. "He said—speaking as your brother— that Jeremy had felt so guilty he gave him this great job, which was why he was in London, which was what took him so long to get here."

She let out a disgusted breath. "London. Big donors to one of his global causes. And a woman, of course. He's got one of those in every port, as they say."

Cooper couldn't say he was surprised, now that it was all unraveling. "Not to mention it explained why he was paying me out of a Brown and Associates account."

"I hope he paid you a lot."

"He did. And he's not getting it back, either."

"Good."

"Speaking as your brother, he said he was totally devoted to you. That he'd never stop looking for you."

"Now that's the first true thing he told you. He would never stop." She lowered her gaze. "He never will."

He lifted a hand, cupped the back of her head, pressed her cheek to his chest. She didn't resist.

"He will," he said.

She gave a tiny, disbelieving shake of her head that he felt as much as saw. Just that she was allowing him to hold her like this amazed him. And now that he knew the truth, it was even more incredible.

"He will, Nell," he said, meaning it more than he'd meant anything since the day he'd made a graveside promise to his father that he'd take care of his mother. "He will, because I'll stop him."

"You can't. No one can."

It was muffled by his shirt, but he still heard the desolation in her voice. He'd done this to her. She'd escaped what he now knew was a horrible situation, after a devastating loss, not to mention the knowledge that the man she'd married had tried to kill her. She'd escaped and built a new life for herself, and he'd destroyed it. The fact that Brown would likely have found her anyway, that if it hadn't been him it would have been someone else who tracked her here, didn't help much. It *had* been him, he was responsible.

Then again, if it hadn't been him, it might have been someone who would have taken Brown at his word, assumed she was unstable, lying, or worse, and who knew what would have happened then. That other guy might have let Brown get away with it, and right now she'd be on her way back into hell.

Instead of here in his arms. Driving him quietly but insistently crazy.

He couldn't stop himself, his arms tightened around her.

"I'll stop him, Nell. I'll find a way. He won't hurt you anymore."

She tilted her head back, looked up at him. He saw the tiniest flicker of hope in her face, nearly crowded out by doubts.

"You'll have to help me," he said. "You'll have to tell me everything you can about him, about his dealings. And then we'll take him down."

"Cooper—"

"We will, Nell. And the bigger he is, well, that just means he's going to fall faster and land harder."

That flicker of hope caught, flared and Cooper felt as if he'd pulled off no small miracle.

And then, because she was a magnet in his arms, with a pull stronger than he could resist, he slowly lowered his head and kissed her.

Chapter 23

Nell's mind was spinning. It had been crazy enough already, but now…

She heard a moan, low and soft. Realized it had risen from her. Felt vaguely like she should be embarrassed, should pull away, but nowhere could she find the strength—or the desire—to do it. The only desire she had was to stay right here, to savor the feel of his arms around her, and to glory in the feel of his mouth on hers.

He'd kissed her before, that afternoon ashore, right here. She'd convinced herself, after, that her fierce response had been born of the circumstances, her fear and isolation and grief. Now she wasn't so sure.

In fact, now she thought she just might be going crazy, at last cracking and turning into that erratic, half-crazy woman Jeremy had accused her of being. Why else would she be out here, on a boat with a man she'd met less than two weeks ago, not only letting him kiss her senseless but reveling in it?

Because she was reveling in it. The hot, firm touch of his lips, the way she could feel his pulse speed up, the way he cupped her face to tilt her head back so he could have more, the way his breathing had quickened as he deepened the kiss, took every bit she offered him even as she was stunned that she was doing it.

Some still-functioning part of her mind was sounding a warning, but the heat that was building in her was unlike anything she'd ever felt, and it was drowning out the warnings of long, hard experience. Once she would have said nothing on earth could ever make her throw caution to the winds again, could ever make her leap without thinking long and hard.

Apparently, Cooper Grant could.

He was pressing her against something hard that dug into her back; she barely noticed. She felt the tentative swipe of his tongue over her lips, and it was the diffidence of it as much as the incredible sensation of him probing, tasting her, that sent her careening down an even more fiery path.

She felt his hands slip down from her face, over her shoulders. They stopped at her waist, shifted her slightly, and suddenly they were pressed together from head to knee. She gasped with the heat of it. He was swamping her, burying her in sensations she'd never known, her head was spinning and she closed her eyes against it but it didn't help, the spinning got faster, tighter, he was surrounding her—

Trapping her.

Panic exploded. Gut-level, unthinking panic. It had nothing to do with him, but she couldn't stop it. She twisted, squirmed, shoved at him. And in the first seconds, when he didn't move, didn't let go, she nearly screamed.

And then she was free.

Cooper stepped back, raising his hands, palms open and facing her in a signal of release. He looked a little dazed, almost bewildered.

But he had let her go.

And now that she could think again, at least a little bit, she could understand his expression. If he'd been feeling anything like she had, caught up in that swirling, hot whirlwind of sensation, it must seem like she'd tossed a bucket of ice water on him.

But he'd stopped. Somehow, he'd understood and stopped.

And perversely, now she felt cold and bereft.

"I'm sorry," he said. He sounded like she felt, with a thick layer of confusion added in. "I thought…I didn't… Hell. I'm sorry."

"Don't."

"I won't. It won't happen again."

"I meant don't apologize."

His brows furrowed. Now he looked thoroughly confused.

"It was…wonderful."

His expression softened. "It was incredible," he said. "Unprofessional, but incredible."

The *incredible* reassured her she hadn't been alone. The *unprofessional* part simply puzzled her. "I'm not your client," she said.

"No, you're not," he said slowly, looking a little relieved. Then, for an instant that anger flashed in his eyes again. "And neither is Brown. As far as I'm concerned, my only client is Tristan Jones. And I'm guessing he'd want me to take care of his sister."

He couldn't have said anything that would have turned her to absolute mush inside faster. If he'd said that before he'd kissed her…

"Cooper," she whispered, wishing she'd never stopped him, that that silly fear hadn't enveloped her, taking over, making her push him away.

For a long moment he stood there silently, studying her. Then, quietly, he said, "I thought you said he wasn't physically abusive."

"He wasn't," she said, understanding his confusion after her reaction. "He never hit me. That would be too unrefined. But he liked to push. Crowd. And then trap me. To remind me that he controlled me. That I could never go anywhere or do anything unless he said so."

Understanding dawned, she could see it cross his face. "I would never—"

She held up her hands much as he had, stopping him. "I know you wouldn't. You just proved that."

For a moment he continued to study her, in that intense, perceptive way that unnerved her a little because he seemed to see so much.

"It was a gut reaction, instinctive," she said, when he didn't speak. "It had nothing to do with you."

"So it wasn't because you hated what I was doing?"

She'd already told him it had been wonderful, but decided he deserved more of a statement. "Hated? Hardly. If it hadn't been so incredible," she said, using his word, "I would have stopped you long before."

A satisfied smile that was so smugly male it made her smile spread across his face. And traces of it remained as he shouldered the duffel that sat on the floor.

"Come on. I'll give you that tour."

He held out his hand to her. She felt the sudden need to show him she'd meant what she'd said, that her moment of panic had nothing to do with him, or not trusting him. Because she did trust him. She wasn't sure exactly when in the past few hours it had happened, but it had.

She immediately took his hand, making her own gesture more pointed than it would have normally been. She saw by the look he gave her then that he understood. He didn't miss much, she thought. No wonder he was good at his job. She even thought that had he met with Jeremy in person, he might just have seen through that formidable facade. And that wasn't something she'd say about many people.

She wondered for a moment what it would be like to live with a man who was that perceptive. She thought it might be a bit disconcerting, but that the benefits might far outweigh the drawbacks.

And then she couldn't believe she was even pondering such

a thing. She crammed the thoughts down into the depths of her mind, telling herself she simply wasn't thinking straight. He was holding her hand, after all.

He led her down a narrow corridor. A door on the left was open, and a glance showed her what appeared to be a workshop equipped with many various tools, a workbench across one wall—were they walls, on boats?—and, oddly, another door on the outside wall. The room smelled faintly of gasoline.

"That's my garage," he said, explaining before she had to ask. "I put in the outside door so I could wheel the bike in and out without tracking it through the main salon."

"Makes sense," she said. Then her eyes widened. "Your motorcycle!"

He shrugged. "Roger will keep an eye on it, I'm sure. Heck, maybe he'll even start riding it."

That image made her smile even as she acknowledged the possibility. "He just might," she said.

She wondered when she'd ever see the man who had been so kind, so generous to her again. If she ever would.

"It won't be long," Cooper said, "and you'll be eating one of his amazing meals, telling him how Jeremy Brown met his downfall at last."

She stared at him. "I could get used to this mind-reading stuff."

He gave her that half shrug again. "It's just noticing. Reading people. And remembering."

"Jeremy does that," she said. Cooper went still, as if she were accusing, and she hastened to go on. "Not the reading people, he's pretty tone-deaf about that. But he does notice and remember."

"I'm not sure I like the comparison."

"It's not a comparison, not really. He uses it for himself, he pays attention so that he can use it on them later. Good or bad, anything and everything is a tool to him. To manipulate.

To charm, or frighten. For you, it's…" Her voice trailed off as she searched for the right words.

"For me, it's just a knack that comes in handy? Is that it?"

"Something like that."

"I can live with that," he said. "Galley you've seen." He made a gesture that included all of the compact but well-equipped space. "Not a whole lot of food. Between Roger and the Waterfront, I've been eating out too much to keep it stocked. Have to go shopping."

The idea of going ashore sent a ripple of that old panic up her spine. How quickly she'd come to think of the boat as a refuge, a safe haven, a place Jeremy couldn't get to. Foolish, nowhere was safe from him, but the illusion was comforting.

He gestured at another small space along the corridor. "Laundry's in there."

"Laundry?"

He tugged a sliding door open, revealing a compact, stacking washer/dryer unit. She shook her head in amazement.

At the back of the boat was a spacious cabin that she guessed was the master stateroom. There were doors along the sides that were probably to closets or other storage, interspersed with portholes that let in a surprising amount of light. Beneath one of the portholes on each side was a built-in bench with a thick cushion, sort of nautical window seats. The bed was a good size, tidily made up and covered with a blue comforter. There were drawers for more storage underneath.

He dropped her duffel atop the blue comforter, then turned to gesture toward a door off to one side.

"Head's in there. Towels in the cabinet behind the door. I just filled the tanks with fresh water, so we should be good for a while. Water heater's small, though, so no twenty-minute hot showers, I'm afraid."

"A hot shower at all is more than I expected," she said.

Cooper grinned at her. Her heart seemed to plummet,

then swoop upward in her chest, taking her ability to breathe properly with it.

"All the comforts of home, for the most part," he said. "Anything you need, ask. I might have it, unless it's seriously girly stuff."

She didn't want to delve into what he meant by that. Or what it meant that whatever he meant by it, he didn't have it aboard. And that thought was so tangled and confused she thought she'd be better off not trying to think at all at the moment.

That kiss probably scrambled your brain, she told herself.

And belatedly she realized that he was talking and acting as if she'd be staying here in this stateroom. Which had to be his. He'd dropped her bag on the bed.

His bed.

Her gaze shot to his face, the memory of that smugly male smile playing back in her head.

"I didn't assume that kiss, hot as it was, was a signal you're ready to sleep with me. No matter how much I wish it had been."

She felt her cheeks heat. "How did you—"

"No perception required on that one, Nell. It was written all over your face."

He disappeared into the bathroom, giving her a chance to regain her composure. Then he reappeared with a razor, shaving cream, a toothbrush and a tube of toothpaste in his hands.

He gestured with the toothpaste. "You have this?"

She nodded, a little numbly. He headed for the doorway. Then he stopped. Turned around. Her breath stopped once more as he looked at her with a heat that matched what she'd felt when he'd kissed her.

"If you change your mind, though," he said, "I'll be right down the hall. Feel free."

One word rose to her lips. It seemed to take everything she had not to speak it, to hold it back until he was gone. She couldn't quite believe how hard it had been. It was only one word. One single syllable, yet she'd had to fight saying it as if a flood of words were piling up on the tip of her tongue.

Just one word she dare not speak, yet had wanted to say with a fierceness that astounded her.

Stay.

Chapter 24

It's your own damn fault. You never should have kissed her.

Cooper's self-lecturing wasn't doing much good. Neither was his determination to just forget about it and get some sleep. And it wasn't just the change of being in the guest stateroom berth, even though it only pounded home the reality of the woman curled up in his bed.

Instead of soothing him as it usually did, the rhythm of the tiny waves slapping against the hull had him thinking of other natural rhythms, like two bodies locked together, finding their own. The cries of the night birds that occasionally split the silence made him think of other cries he'd have liked to hear in the night, from the woman sleeping—probably soundly—just yards away.

He rolled over yet again, slamming his fist into his pillow as if the helpless sack of feathers were somehow responsible for his sleeplessness.

"Your own damned fault," he muttered into the darkness.

He took some small comfort in the truth of what she'd said; she wasn't his client. There would have been no way past that one. He'd said that everyone had a code, whether they admitted it or not. And kissing a client while she was a client was not in his. Sleeping with her would be…

Incredible.

He shook his head sharply. Maybe she wasn't a client, but she was the center of this case. Except, did he even have a case, when the person who hired him had lied from the get-go? When the person who hired him had not only done it under false pretenses, but with nefarious intent?

When the person who hired him had tried to kill her? And had killed her beloved brother?

The image formed in his mind, so vivid it was as if he'd been there. He could picture so well what had happened that night: Jeremy Brown coming upon his wife and her brother, gathering up what was most precious to her. That would have signaled to him what was impending, that she was about to make a break, to free herself from his grasp. Whether he'd come armed, honestly thinking about a burglar, or gone for the weapon when he'd seen what was going on, didn't really matter at this point. What mattered was that he'd come after them with the weapon.

And Tristan Jones had done what he'd apparently done all their lives; he'd protected his little sister. He'd put himself between them, in the line of fire.

Cooper knew how fast things happened in situations like that. Most civilians took so long to process what was actually happening that they ended up dead. Which told him that Tristan had not been caught by surprise. He'd known Brown was a threat, had to have suspected he might do something drastic when he realized he was about to lose his prized possession.

Any step out of line or inappropriate word spoken required atonement in his world. And filing for divorce certainly fell into that category.

Her words echoed in his head. Why had Brown waited until that night? Had he not believed she'd really have the nerve until he saw her packing up her things?

You underestimated her, he thought.

And he had the feeling that the man, for all his power, always had. He thought he'd married a quiet, malleable, obedient little sparrow. And Nell—Tanya, then—had been vulnerable, weakened by grief and loss and thought she'd found refuge.

But even that sparrow had a breaking point. And then she had blossomed into a hawk.

He felt a burst of warmth that it took him a moment to recognize. Pride. He was proud of that little sparrow, of the hawk she'd become. And she should be proud of herself. Sometime, when she might listen, he'd point that out.

In the meantime, he'd better keep his emotions—and his suddenly unruly body—in check.

He had a little success in the sleep department, not so much in the controlling urges department, by the time dawn crept over the mountains. Tonight, he told himself, he'd sleep up in the pilot's berth, away from temptation. Then laughed inwardly; he couldn't get far enough away for that if *The Peacemaker* were a hundred-footer.

After a rough night of self-recriminations, he figured he might as well finish the job. He got up and walked out to get his phone. With no WiFi connection for his laptop out here, he'd have to use the smartphone for this. He sat down at the table adjacent to the galley and began the research he should have done long ago.

He had to quash that little voice that nagged at him, telling him what he already knew quite well: that he should have done this long ago. He should have known that what had seemed so clear-cut and simple might not be, he should have remembered one of the first rules of any investigation: people lie.

A while later he had the basics. And looking at it all dispassionately, he wondered if he would have tumbled to the lie even if he had done his homework when he should have. He'd never seen Brown in person before he'd turned up yesterday, so he wouldn't have known what he looked like to compare to the photographs he'd found of the man. There were a couple of video news clips from after the shooting, brief statements Brown had made. Perhaps if he'd listened to them rather than just reading the transcriptions, he might have recognized his voice.

Maybe.

But the things he couldn't deny would have changed everything were the various reports confirming that Tristan Jones had been pronounced dead on the scene. And there was nothing, anywhere, of a miraculous revival by paramedics or emergency room staff—and that, Cooper knew, was something that would hardly go unnoticed in the flurry of news covering the story.

Because Jeremy Brown was exactly what Nell had said he was. Powerful. Big-time. Famous. Newsworthy.

If nothing else, that had become clear in the stories he'd scanned. Since her brother, not her husband, had hired him—or so he'd thought—he'd stopped after the initial coverage. If it had been the husband looking for her, he would have been suspicious, but the brother…somehow it seemed more innocent.

So he hadn't done his homework. And Nell had paid the price for it.

"Cooper?"

The sound of his name in her soft, sleepy voice blasted away all the fine shoring up he'd done. He pasted a smile on his face and turned to look at her, knowing he'd regret it. Knowing he'd want nothing more than to take her right back to bed.

She'd left the glasses behind. Without the heavy frames to mask her face, he could see the delicate structure of her face. He'd seen her without them only a couple of times, and it always struck him what an effective disguise they were.

She'd dressed in her usual jeans but wore a blue, long-sleeved, lightweight sweater. No shoes, only matching, heavy blue socks.

"Are you cold?" he asked, looking at the sweater and trying not to focus solely on curves usually hidden by the loose T-shirts she favored. "I can kick up the heat."

She blinked. "There's a heater?"

He grinned. "Forced air, and air-conditioning, too, in case of a run to the tropics. All the comforts of home."

"Oh. Nice."

She walked toward him, brushing a stray lock of hair back from her forehead. Her hair was a little tousled, and her eyes—

Were blue. A bright, vivid, startling blue.

"No wonder you went with the brown contacts," he said. "Your eyes would be…hard to forget."

She looked at the floor, as if she were self-conscious—or worried—about the lack of camouflage. "It's nice not to have to mess with them."

"So you don't really need them or the glasses at all?"

She shook her head. Yawned.

"Did you sleep?"

Her gaze lifted to his face. "I did," she said, sounding somewhat surprised. "The water, the sounds…I thought it would all keep me awake, but I slept."

Unlike me, he thought. Obviously she hadn't been tormented with the same kind of thoughts he had. Figured. Why would she be when, from her point of view, he'd ruined everything for her?

"Good," he said, his thoughts making his voice a little brusque. "Hungry?"

"Not really, not yet."

"Coffee's on. Won't be as good as the café's, but it's hot and full of caffeine."

"Thanks. I—" Her words broke off abruptly. "The café," she whispered.

He'd been expecting this. She'd had some sleep now, was in a fairly safe place, off Brown's radar, so now her mind turned to the fallout. She was starting to realize that her world had been shattered yet again. Yesterday the fear had carried her through, the need for haste had prevented her from dwelling on it. This morning, all that was gone, leaving her with nothing but the grim facts.

"You were leaving anyway," he said.

"But not like this. I was going to—"

"Say goodbye?" He stood up, closed the three feet between them in a single stride. "Better to wait, and say hello again when you go back."

She shivered. And he couldn't help himself, he put his arms around her, wanting to share warmth, to stop that faint trembling that shook him to his soul.

And he took heart from the simple fact that she didn't push him away. "You make it sound possible," she whispered.

"It is. It will be."

She shook her head in disbelief. He didn't try to convince her, not now. He sensed she was still too shaken by her ex— hell, that's what he was—showing up when she thought she was safe to believe anything good right now.

The logistics of getting away had distracted her yesterday, he thought. Maybe more logistics would help today. He held on to her one last moment, savoring the feel of her in his arms, then let go.

"There's that little grocery just outside the park," he said. "I thought I'd go stock up."

"Go?"

She looked startled, even scared. He wasn't foolish enough to think she was sorry he'd let go of her, or even that she'd miss him while he was gone. She was just wary of being alone right now, with Brown out there, somewhere.

"I'm thinking you should stay here," he said. "Not be seen. I don't think he's going to find us anytime soon, but it's best to be cautious."

He heard her take in a deep breath, as if she were trying to steady herself.

"All right," she said after a moment.

Her voice was solid, strong. And it had taken her only moments. She was finding herself again.

"Give me a list of anything you want. Don't know if they'll have it, but I'll look. Better grab the chance now."

"How long?"

His brow furrowed. "How long will it take, or how long should you stock up for?"

Her mouth quirked. "Yes."

He couldn't help grinning at her. "I should only be gone an hour or so."

She frowned. It was disconcerting, seeing her eyes, he'd gotten so used to them being that medium brown that the bright blue was still a shock.

"How will you carry it all?"

He smiled as her mind turned to the practicalities first. She had her fear under control now, he thought.

"I've got a big backpack. Between that and what bags I can carry, I should be able to get all we need. Unless you want wine every night."

She shook her head, then went still. "Every night? So stock up for a long stay?"

"Better safe," he said. "Who knows how long we'll need to figure out a way to take him down?"

Her breath caught audibly. "You sound so positive."

"I am. There's a way, we just have to find it."

"But he's—"

"I know what he is." He grimaced. "This morning I did the homework I should have done before."

"Then you know. He's untouchable."

"No one's untouchable. At least, no one swimming in the ponds he frequents. There will be something. Some way." He still saw doubt clearly in her face. "But for now, let's just get organized. Then when you're ready, we'll start brainstorming."

"You really think we have time?"

"Some, yes. If Roger's misdirection worked, that'll really slow him down. He might eventually find out about *The Peacemaker,* but that'll take him more time."

"He doesn't know you live on a boat?"

He shook his head, one corner of his mouth twisting upward

wryly. "Some people don't take you seriously if you don't have an office, an assistant and a ton of file cabinets, so I don't make a habit of advertising it."

She tilted her head slightly, giving him a quizzical look. "You don't like offices?"

He started to make his standard joke about office walls being the same as house walls, and that he preferred to be free of both. And it was true, as far as it went. But something about the way she was looking at him, or perhaps simply that it was her, made him give her the bare bones facts.

"I can afford an office, or I can keep *The Peacemaker*. I can't do both."

"And *The Peacemaker* is more important to you."

"Yes."

"Because it was your father's."

"She was his dream. He wanted to sail her around the world when he retired."

Her brows rose. She looked around at the interior of the vessel. "And your mom was up for that?"

"Not so much, but she would have done it," he said. "She always said wherever he was was home for her."

She blinked, then again, more rapidly, and he thought he saw the sheen of moisture in those very blue eyes. "That's…"

She didn't finish, as if words had failed her.

"Love," he said. "They had something special."

She lapsed into silence, but he could see in her face she was thinking of how it had ended, how tragedy had destroyed that love.

"Is it worth it?" she said, almost to herself.

"I don't know," he answered.

It was a question he'd wrestled with ever since he'd been old enough to understand the magnitude of losing someone you loved like that.

It was a question his mother would unfailingly answer *Yes*.

It was a question he couldn't answer at all. Because he didn't know if he was even capable of loving someone like that.

And that he was even thinking about it made him restless. Almost as restless as spending the night just a few feet away from Nell. Because he had the uneasy feeling she was the reason his mind was delving into areas he was more comfortable ignoring.

The simple fact was that he was so hot for her he was surprised the sound wasn't boiling around them.

Chapter 25

This was crazy, Nell thought, as she tore lettuce into pieces.

Jeremy was out there somewhere, moving whatever mountains his money could move to find her. Yet they were just sitting here, as if they were on some kind of boating vacation, as if they had all the time in the world. Cooper was puttering around in the galley, getting ready to grill steaks on the small barbecue that was fastened to one of the railings on the outside deck at the stern of *The Peacemaker*.

He'd said nothing more about their situation all day. And if she tried to bring it up, he hushed her with a quiet but definite "Later." And had continued on as if this was nothing more than an enjoyable interlude.

Not that it wasn't pleasant. In fact, it was downright soothing. There was a feeling of safety in being offshore. It was as if the water was their own private moat, protecting the floating castle from invaders.

Or dragons.

It was the most whimsical thought she'd had in years, and it made her smile. But reality was still out there, and she knew if she forgot that safety was an illusion, she might relearn the lesson the hard way. The hardest possible way.

What if what had happened at the cottage yesterday had turned ugly, had turned into a replay of what had happened that night months ago? Cooper had stood with her, had intervened, and if Jeremy had been armed, as he had been that night, it could have ended up much the same way.

Unless…did he have a weapon himself? She'd seen no sign of one, but he was a private investigator—didn't they have them? Of course, he'd said "Of sorts." Did that mean he didn't have the licenses and permits necessary?

"I like the first thought better."

She nearly jumped as he spoke from bare inches behind her. "What?"

"The one that made you smile."

She let out a self-disgusted breath. She'd been lost in her musings, not a wise path when you had someone like Jeremy on your trail.

"Silliness," she said.

"I think you're overdue for a little silliness. What was it?"

She glanced around, gesturing at the large windows and the water outside. "Castles and moats," she said.

"And safety?" he asked quietly, clearly remembering what she'd once said to him about the illusion.

"And dragons," she said, and it wasn't at all amusing this time.

"Dragons still have to find you," he said. "And even dragons have their vulnerabilities. Otherwise there'd be more of them. You'd be running into them on every street corner."

For an instant she just gaped at him. The image he'd just planted in her head was irresistible. He grinned as if he knew it. And for the first time in longer than she could remember, she honestly, openly and thoroughly laughed.

"Now that," Cooper said with obvious satisfaction, "is a sound worth slaying dragons for."

She felt her cheeks heat. She'd thought herself long beyond blushing, thought her life with Jeremy had beaten the reaction out of her, yet this man had made her do it twice in less than twenty-four hours.

And as he walked out onto the deck, she busied herself with the salad she'd been making, trying not to think of the last time he'd done it. Last night.

I didn't assume that kiss, hot as it was, was a signal you're ready to sleep with me. No matter how much I wish it had been.

A shiver rippled through her, a shiver that had nothing to do with air temperature and everything to do with the blast of heat that shot through her, radiating out from some deeply buried place she had thought long dead.

Would he laugh if he knew the real reason she'd slept last night was the faint scent of him in the cabin, in his bed? If he knew how she'd wrapped it around her unsettled mind and calmed herself with it?

If he knew how much she had wanted to accept that invitation, how much she wished she could "feel free" enough to go to him? How she'd actually ached for him, in a way she'd never known?

He might not laugh—he wasn't a cruel man—but it was certainly laugh-worthy. Was she still that weak, that foolish, that she would once again turn to the nearest strong man for shelter, protection?

Not that Cooper was anything like Jeremy. He wasn't. But that didn't mean she wasn't turning to him for the same reasons. The fault was in her, not him. She was looking for safety again, and it didn't exist. Hadn't she learned that yet?

Of course, there was that little matter of heat and need and a body suddenly in overdrive. Now *that* was new. That, she'd never felt in her life before. Had thought it was a creation of human imagination, over the eons. Until now.

And she didn't want to think about it from his side. Why the interest in the plain little thing she'd made herself into? Even without the purposely unflattering glasses, the image she'd met in the mirror this morning, weary eyes, no makeup, wasn't in the least eye-catching to her. Of course, guys looked at it differently, didn't they? Maybe he just wanted sex with her because she was female, and handy. Maybe he just wanted sex with her because he just wanted sex.

That was all it could be, really. Wasn't it?

She hadn't really been watching what she was doing, but suddenly the salad bowl came into focus, and she realized that if she didn't stop, they'd be eating coleslaw-style lettuce, she was shredding it so finely.

She stopped, put her hands down on the counter. The galley—she knew that much, at least—was compact, room for two people only if they were intimate enough that they would have shared that bed last night.

She looked around for something to do, to distract her from being alone. They had hand-washed the dishes from last night—the boat held three hundred gallons, Cooper had said, and there was a water maker, a small desalinization plant aboard—but still no need to be profligate when they weren't at a dock and hooked up to shore supplies, and needed to take showers and such.

She could do that, she thought. While he was gone. Except… if something happened, she'd be beyond vulnerable, naked and wet. She should wait until Cooper was back.

Oh, yes, do that. Wait until he's back on board to get naked and wet.

The image and all the possible meanings sent ripples of alternating heat and chill through her until she thought she might truly be going insane.

She hurried down the corridor to the master stateroom he'd given over to her. She could have easily stayed in the smaller guest quarters; it was just as nicely turned out, merely smaller. But the head was across the hall instead of directly attached, so the master gave her more privacy. It had been a thoughtful gesture, one that Jeremy certainly never would have made. He would have kept the best for himself and always had.

As she investigated the workings, then showered, she thought about how her world had truly been turned inside out. She never would have imagined ending up on a boat at all, let alone one anchored nowhere near anything she knew.

She'd gone from one life, where change was to be avoided, living with a man who liked everything just so, to building a life of her own where she—

She abruptly stopped her own thoughts. But she couldn't deny what would have come next: a life of her own where she liked everything just so. And was wary—no, downright afraid—of changes.

She finished briskly, tried to focus on drying off and getting dressed quickly. But the thoughts remained, circling, demanding to be faced.

So what had she gained? True, she'd been out from under Jeremy's thumb, but if she just re-created the same kind of carefully unchanging life, what had she done except change masters?

And now she was tangled up with a guy who thrived on change. Who moved around like some restless vagabond, who had no roots, nothing but an anchor that held him in one place for a while but could be lifted at any moment to move on.

She walked across the salon to where there were three pictures fastened between two of the big windows. The top one was of a man in the pilothouse, sitting at the big wheel, with a young boy on his lap. The man was looking back over his shoulder at the photographer, a smile of pure joy on his face. A smile reminiscent of the killer grin of his son—who, in the photograph, was looking up at his father with nothing short of adoration. The man had one hand on the wheel, and his other arm was wrapped securely and protectively around the boy, who looked to be about twelve in the picture.

The pang at the future that lay ahead so soon for that loving pair made her close her eyes. She wondered how Cooper stood it, having that reminder here every day. Then she realized his father had probably put it there himself, and Cooper certainly wasn't going to change it. And maybe it had always been there, so he didn't really see it, the way people never saw things they walked by every day.

She opened her eyes, but looked at the second picture this time. It didn't help much; it was a young man in a police uniform, looking stern as such pictures always seemed to, posed in front of a flowing American flag. There was an undeniable resemblance between father and son, especially visible in this photo, where she guessed he was a little younger than Cooper was now. She wondered how his mother felt, looking at him and seeing so much of the man she'd loved in the son left behind. Did she take solace in it, or was it a painful reminder of a love lost?

Both, she thought, remembering how seeing the traces of their mother in Tristan's green eyes and auburn hair had both comforted her and made her feel the occasional ache of loss. She herself took after their father, something she had tried to ignore since the day he'd vanished from their lives. She tried, and mostly succeeded, in never thinking about him at all.

She shifted her gaze to the third and last photograph. Cooper, dressed in graduation robes, in front of the roaring cougar symbol of Washington State University. He was standing next to a petite, slender woman dressed in a pale green suit and wearing a smile full of pride tinged with wistfulness. Around them in a half circle were three men, all with the same air of competence and toughness.

She studied the faces, the expressions that seemed to hold a combination of sadness and satisfaction. Similar to the look on the woman's face. Pride in her son, obviously, but also sadness that his father wasn't there to see this day.

"My surrogate fathers."

Cooper's voice came from so close behind her she did jump this time. God, she'd been so oblivious she hadn't even heard him board. True, he moved with amazing silence when he wanted to—another trick of the trade, she supposed—but you'd think she would have at least heard something.

He set down the stuffed backpack and the two large bags

he'd come back with. He walked over to stand beside her. It didn't do much to calm the startled racing of her pulse.

"One on the left is Dave Lindsey, my dad's partner when he went down. Next is their boss, Lieutenant Pinsky, he's a captain now. Then Chuck Hernandez, my dad's first partner on the force, who retired a couple of years before Dad was killed."

She was steadier now, although still mentally chastising herself for getting so lost in her thoughts she'd been taken unaware. What if it had been Jeremy?

"Surrogate fathers?" she asked.

"They all pitched in. Stayed involved in our lives. Helped my mom when she needed it, and when I needed it. Helped me with sports, or chewed me out if I was straying off the path."

"That's wonderful."

"It was a pact they made. A cop thing. That if anything happened to one of the four, the other three would see to their family."

She couldn't imagine living like that, with what to most people would be an abstract, remote chance being an absolute and very real possibility.

"That's even more wonderful," she said quietly.

"They're good guys. We all still get together on Dad's birthday. And I know if my mother needed anything I couldn't handle, they'd be there."

That made her shift her gaze to the woman in the picture. "She's lovely," she said.

"Yes."

"She must have been so proud that day."

"As opposed to now?"

She flushed. "I didn't mean it that way."

"Why not? Most women do. Rootless, drifter, immature, homeless, that's the general riff."

"You're not homeless." She gestured around at the cabin. "I was just thinking earlier, if you count it all, this isn't much smaller than my first apartment. Besides, if you really wanted to be completely rootless, you'd have a sailboat, like you said. Not tied to anything."

He blinked, as if he were startled that she'd used his own thoughts back at him.

"And I think wanting to hang on to your father's dream is admirable," she added. "As long as you love it, too."

"I do love it."

He was looking at her with that intensity that made her edgy. And she was surprised at herself, at the way that defense had leaped to her lips without a thought. Especially since, in the beginning, she'd thought the same way those women he'd quoted had felt.

And now, she didn't want to think about those women at all, whoever they'd been. Didn't want to think about him being with them.

Any of them, she guessed, wouldn't have kept him sleeping down the hall. Which made who the fool? Them? Or her?

And then he tossed the bucket of cold water that shocked her out of the haze of heated musings she'd been mired in since last night.

"What about your father, Nell?"

Chapter 26

Nell visibly stiffened. "What about him? He walked out on us, and never came back."

There was anger and bitterness in her voice.

"When?"

She shrugged, as if it didn't matter anymore. But he knew better; you weren't angry or bitter if you didn't care.

"The day after my eighteenth birthday. Tris was nineteen, twenty in another month. My father said he'd gotten us that far, now it was up to us."

"Cold."

"Yes. And I don't talk about it."

"You should."

She made a muttered sound that somehow managed to express rather eloquently what she thought of that opinion.

"It'll just eat you alive, Nell. Bitterness is an acid that'll eat you up from the inside out."

"Right."

"Trust me, I know what I'm talking about. It almost did me in. After my dad was killed I was so angry, so bitter, that I was headed down a very wrong path. Getting in all kinds of trouble."

She gave him a sideways glance then, and he saw that she

was at least listening. He gestured at the graduation photo, at the man on the far end.

"Dave got wind of it. My mom probably called him, because I wasn't listening to her. He tracked me down. Took me out to the middle of nowhere, chewed me a new one. Told me I was betraying my father's memory, and that he'd be ashamed of me. Making my mom worry and all. Then he told me to think about it until he came back in the morning."

She blinked. "He left you there? All night?"

He nodded. "Miles from anywhere. Left me a bottle of water. I spent the night pretty cold, hungry and miserable." His mouth quirked. "And a little scared. They don't call them the Washington State Cougars for nothing."

She shivered. "That's awful."

"Tough love," he said. "And it worked. I'd been so angry and bitter that he was gone that I never thought about what my father would think of the way I was acting."

He saw her expression change. "So I'm supposed to forgive him?"

"Did your mother love him?" he asked, dodging the question with one of his own.

"Yes. And to be fair," she said, almost reluctantly, "he stuck with her throughout her illness. He did everything for her."

She sounded as if she hadn't thought about that in a long time. He supposed it was too painful to dwell on, a feeling he understood all too well himself.

"So he loved her," he said.

She nodded. "That we never doubted."

"You just don't think he loved you."

"Not enough to stay."

"But he did stay. Until you were legally an adult."

"He had to, didn't he?"

He let that go. He wasn't even sure why he was pursuing this, except it seemed important. And he'd been there. "Don't you think he trusted your brother to look out for you if you needed it?"

She blinked. "He knew Tris would always take care of me." She seemed to hear how that sounded, and added, "In an emergency, I mean. I didn't need a…keeper."

Her hesitation before the last word told him she knew that was exactly what she'd gone for with Jeremy Brown. She didn't need him pointing out the obvious. So he went for the money point instead.

"What would your mother think of how you feel about him? How you blame him?"

"She would have wanted him to take care of her children!"

"And he did. He didn't walk out when he probably wanted to, Nell. He stayed, fighting his own pain, until you were old enough to take care of yourself. And you had your brother as…insurance."

She stared at him. Something he'd said had gotten to her, he could see it. He just didn't know what it was.

"His own pain," she whispered.

He seized on it. "You think you and your brother were the only ones hurting? My mother always said kids are only yours for a while, then they're off to make their own lives. Your mate is the one who's forever. Or is supposed to be. Lose that, and it's like losing a big chunk of yourself. And all of your future."

She gave a tiny, choked cry, then she spun on her heel and ran, vanishing into the master stateroom and closing the door sharply behind her.

"Nice work, Grant," he muttered.

He busied himself putting away the things he'd bought. The small store's selection had been mainly basics, with the addition of some local seafood that looked tempting. There was room in the small freezer, so he'd bought enough to provide a nice variety, along with some other meats. He'd never shopped for two on a regular basis, so it was a bit of a novelty for him.

To his own surprise he enjoyed it, and it kept him distracted from the promise he'd made, perhaps rather rashly. Just because his father had helped take down one of the biggest drug operations in the state didn't mean he had the same ability. And just because his father had once won a medal of valor for rescuing a woman and two children from a burning house didn't mean he could rescue this one from her powerful soon-to-be-ex, he thought, recognizing wryly that he seemed bent on referring to Brown that way.

He wasn't his father. He wasn't some larger-than-life hero, respected by all and loved by many. He was just a boat bum who played at being a detective, respected by few and loved by fewer. Mom aside, of course. But that was kind of in her job description.

"Did you ever want to be a cop, like your dad?"

He'd heard the sound of her sock-clad feet, so he wasn't startled by her approach. He was startled by the question. Enough to answer honestly.

"Always."

"Then why didn't you?"

He gestured at the bottom photograph. "My mother. She made me promise. From the time he died, she made me promise every year, on his birthday."

"Not to become a cop?"

He nodded. "It was the only thing she ever asked of me. Under the circumstances, I couldn't say no. It was the only thing I could do to make her happy."

"But if it was your dream…"

He shrugged. "She might have let up, later. She even told me, a couple of years ago, that she shouldn't have forced that on me. But by then, it was already out of my head as an impossibility." He'd had enough of the subject, so he slid into a joke. "Along with nuclear physicist, brain surgeon and president."

She smiled, albeit halfheartedly. "Because?"

"Not smart enough, not careful enough, not ambitious enough."

"Ambition builds countries. Blind ambition destroys them," she said.

He blinked. "Who said that?"

"I'm not sure if anybody real did. I read it in a novel." She looked down, studying her toes for a moment. Then she took a breath and looked back at him. "I'm sorry."

He'd put his foot in it, and she was apologizing to him?

"I've always been so angry at him that I never really thought about it from his side. And I think I even blamed him, partially, for Mom dying. He should have saved her. That kind of childish thing."

"That's normal."

"Like you thinking you should have saved your father? Somehow kept him from being in that store that day?"

He nodded.

"But you got over that."

"Eventually. In my head. My gut, sometimes not so much."

She gave him a look that was almost grateful for that. "I didn't. I let my emotional reaction stay what it had been when she died. And when he left, it just seemed to validate my feelings. He didn't care, he never had."

"And it never occurred to you that maybe he cared too much?"

She sighed. "No. He tried to explain, but I wouldn't listen. And now—" she gave an embarrassed shrug "—I've done what he did. I ran. You'd think I would have understood better how he felt."

"When he left, were you all right? I mean, he didn't leave you out on the street, did he?"

"No. He had inherited some money from his father. Quite a bit, actually. He left it in trust for us, with Tris as trustee. The monthly amount was more than enough, until we got going on our own."

"So he didn't really abandon you."

She sighed again. Her face showed the torment she'd been through, then and now. It was startling how much the glasses and even the dark contacts had masked; now it seemed her every emotion was there in her eyes.

"No. He didn't. He just escaped an intolerable situation."

"Did you ever hear from him?"

"For a while. Cards on our birthdays. From all over the country. I burned mine."

"Unopened, I presume."

This time the sigh was accompanied by a grimace. "I was an angry, scared, immature kid. I know that. What's so wrong, and so pitiful, was I let my emotions about him freeze there. I hung on to that sense of betrayal and abandonment, long after I should have outgrown it."

"I was angry at my dad, too. For leaving me."

"But he had no choice. Mine did," she pointed out. Then the grimace again. "See? It's ingrained."

"Let it go, Nell. You know you have to. You've known for a long time."

She frowned. "What makes you think that?"

"You wouldn't have gotten there so quickly just now, if you hadn't already been there on some level."

She looked doubtful, then thoughtful, as if she'd realized there was truth in what he'd said.

"Thank you," she said, her voice soft.

"My mom always said there's absolutely no point in going through hell unless you can later show someone else the way."

"Your mom sounds wonderful."

"She is. You'd like her, I think."

Nell glanced at the photograph. "So do I."

"When this is over," he began. Then he stopped, realizing what he'd almost said, that he'd like her to meet his mother. He nearly groaned at what he'd let slip into his thinking, that there would still be a connection between them when this was over.

"So whose fault was your brother's death?" he said abruptly, almost harshly.

She drew back sharply at the unexpected offensive. He'd meant it to shock, to distract from his own floundering, but the look on her face made him feel like he'd slapped her. As, figuratively, he supposed he had.

"I just thought while you were reapportioning guilt, you might have made some changes there, too," he said, trying to say it lightly enough to blunt the initial impact.

For a moment she simply looked at him, and he was utterly unable to read her expression. Then she gave a sharp nod.

"I have. I know whose fault it was. Tris died protecting me, but not because of me. That lies completely at Jeremy's feet."

He let out a relieved breath. "You've been working on that in the back of your mind, too, haven't you?"

"I must have been," she agreed. "Or like you said, I wouldn't have gotten there so quickly now. Nor would I," she said, holding his gaze levelly, "without you. Thank you. You're a remarkable man, Cooper Grant. No matter what you might think."

He felt suddenly awkward.

And suddenly, fiercely hot.

"Don't look at me like that," he muttered.

"Like what?"

"Like you wish you'd come down the hall last night."

"I do."

He blinked. Struggled for air that seemed suddenly in short supply. If she hadn't looked so startled at her own temerity, he doubted if he could have gotten a word out.

"We could make up for that now," he said, hardly recognizing the thickness of his own voice.

He heard her breath catch. "You're sure you want to?"

Given he'd been battling images of this incessantly, he nearly groaned aloud. "Isn't that supposed to be my question?"

"I don't know. Is it?"

For a moment he thought she was teasing. Then he realized she was honestly asking. And he vowed in that moment that, if nothing else, he was going to make sure that she didn't think of that bastard she'd married once when she was in his arms.

And then she was, and Cooper's body responded with a speed that jolted him; it had already gotten the message that the battle was over, that this time the images would be made reality.

By the time they got to the stateroom he knew he was in overdrive, and tried desperately to slow down. What small part of his logical brain that was still functioning knew he had to go slow, knew that she had to know every step of this was at her pace, her choosing. She'd had too few choices before, he was going to give her all of them now. Even if it killed him.

Which, he thought as he tugged at her shirt, it just might.

But she didn't seem inclined to let him go slow. Or perhaps it was just that he was so revved up it seemed every move he made she countered with her own. When he slipped off her shirt, he barely had a moment to savor, then tamp down the fierce heat that rose in him at the sight of the luscious curve of her breasts, so often hidden by the excess cloth. Because she was tugging at his shirt in turn. In the process her fingers brushed over the bare skin of his belly, and every muscle beneath them clenched so hard he could barely breathe.

He unhooked her bra, spilling perfectly shaped breasts tipped with pink loose to tempt his hands. But even as their softness rounded into his hands he lost his breath again as she reached for his waistband. She fumbled for a moment, but then she had the button undone, and the restraint of denim eased as she unzipped him.

He barely had the determination to get out the words he knew he needed to say.

"You want to stop, say so. Whenever."

In answer she slid her hands around to his hips and began to push his jeans downward.

Things happened fast after that. And he gave up any pretense of going slow.

"Next time," he muttered as they went down to the berth

in a tangle of naked limbs and gasping breaths. "Next time, slow."

He tried, genuinely tried to keep some tiny bit of focus on any signals she might give him, that she wanted to stop, that she'd changed her mind, but thinking wasn't something his brain did very well when every bit of blood and every nerve in his body was occupied elsewhere.

And then she was touching him, caressing his aroused flesh with such a gentle, hesitant motion that it was all he could do to hold back. He groaned her name, clutching at the pillow beneath her head, grasping for any kind of control. But then he reached down, touched her, found her slick and wet, heard her tiny gasp as he brushed over that knot of nerves. He circled, pressed, stroked until she was arching to his touch.

And then he ran completely out of restraint. He shifted over her, grateful when she opened for him, beyond grateful when she guided him home.

It was so hot, so intense, if the chilly sound was boiling around them it wouldn't have surprised him. And when she moaned his name, when he felt her body tighten around him, felt the rhythmic clenching, he let himself go with a groan of her name that broke from a place so deep and protected he felt as if he'd been simultaneously ripped apart and made whole.

Chapter 27

"There has to be something we can use against him. What about the affairs?"

Nell shrugged. "There were dozens, I'm sure. Five that I know who they are."

"Any proof?"

"Nothing I was able to bring with me," she said, her tone wry but her voice steady.

That he was touching her, idly—or seemingly idly—stroking the back of her hand with his fingers, helped. They sat across the polished table from each other, Cooper with a yellow legal pad in front of him for notes. Not the kind she would normally make, an orderly list, but rather a diagram of sorts, a starburst of lines and names and locations and events, all leading inward to where he'd written "Brown" in dark, jagged, almost Gothic-looking letters.

She had thought, when she'd still been able to think at all where he was concerned, that he would be either a very casual or a very intense lover. It had turned out he was both. Casually able to laugh at the awkwardness of their first time together, relieving her embarrassment—and her fear that he'd regret this, that she was, in fact, inadequate—yet so intense once they'd found the rhythm that suited them that she'd felt seared to the core.

And he assured her in a way words never could that Jeremy's cool dismissal of her desirability in bed was born of his problems in that arena, not hers.

"Besides," she said, "in the circles he runs in, affairs are almost a given. A résumé enhancement, in fact. He'd pretend embarrassment, give a good show of contrition, but given his crazy loon of a wife, it would be, of course, understandable that he looked elsewhere."

He gave those last words such a scornful expression of disgust that it warmed her all over again.

"Straight affairs?" he asked.

"What?"

"Is he gay?"

She wondered for a moment if there was a compliment for her in there, that Jeremy would have to be gay not to find her desirable. Then she nearly laughed aloud at herself; after the afternoon they'd just spent in the master stateroom, she shouldn't have any doubts left, or any need for compliments. Not from this man, who had practically worshipped her into oblivion for hours.

"No, I don't think so. I just think Jeremy's only capacity for love is spent on himself. Something I was thankful for, since it meant he didn't come to me very often."

"Good," he said bluntly, and again she felt warmed. "All right. Something else then. If we can't use sex, then money."

"Meaning?"

"Any donations, or donors, who might be suspect? In any way?"

Nell smothered a sigh and began to search her memory. They'd been at this for hours now. And all the while a good portion of her mind—and all of her sated yet eager for more body—was yearning to go back to bed. With him. For the next month or so.

She'd worried, at first, that he'd find her too needy, too eager, too desperate. But that had been when she could still think at all, a situation he took care of the moment he'd had her naked and begun to explore every inch of her, in a way that made her feel as if she were some as-yet-undiscovered paradise.

And the discovery was the most amazing thing she'd ever experienced.

She yanked her mind back to the matter at hand, and to what he was saying.

"—anything like that?"

"I'm sorry," she said. "I was…daydreaming."

His gaze came up from the legal pad to her face. And whatever he read there made him smile in a very satisfied, very male way. But thankfully for her already overheated cheeks, he didn't pursue it.

"I was asking," he said in a voice that made her feel as if he hadn't had to pursue it because he knew exactly where her mind had wandered, "if there was anything he really seemed eager to hide. Activities, meetings he wanted to keep secret, phone calls, anything."

"He *did* hide almost everything from me. He would tell me he had a meeting, but never where or with who."

"What about all the fundraising functions?"

"At public events, I was to be charming, gracious, the image of the perfect wife. The hair, the makeup, it all had to be perfect." She ran a hand through her already tousled hair. "This is almost my natural color now. I hated being a blonde."

She waited, half-expecting him to say he wished she'd go back. He didn't.

"It suits you" was all he said.

Mollified, she went on. "He spent a lot of money on a wardrobe picked out by a professional stylist, but if I ever wore something he didn't like, it was my fault, not hers."

He made a gruff, disgusted sound that even further eased her mind. "What about at his office? He had one, didn't he?"

"I was never allowed at his office unless he summoned me."

"Summoned?"

Her mouth twisted. "He never simply asked. It was always a summons. Not that it was very often. Maybe two or three times. I was too stupid to be of much use, and too unstable to be trusted with his precious business."

A snort of laughter burst from him, a sound that soothed her so much it was startling.

"Why would he call you in at all, then?" he asked.

She shrugged. "Usually there was a woman involved, a donor he thought would respond best to his facade of devoted husband."

"Devoted, huh?"

"Of course. Why else would he tolerate my many flaws? That was always his subtext."

Cooper shook his head slowly. "Damn. Lucky you didn't have kids. He probably would have completely warped them."

"I made sure that never happened, because he made it quite clear to me that if I ever got pregnant, an abortion would happen the next day. To the world, of course, he wanted children, he loved children and it was my fault we couldn't have them."

For a moment he just looked at her, and then he asked the question she dreaded, the question she'd tried to answer so often herself.

"Why did you stick it out as long as you did?"

She let out a weary sigh. "I've spent months trying to figure that out. I was so weak, in the beginning. At first it was so good to feel safe again that I took his overcontrol as caring. When it got worse, I told myself that it was still better than that lost, alone feeling I had after losing Mom, then my father, in so short a time."

He seemed to hesitate, then asked, "What about your brother? Did he know?"

"Not for a long time. Tris had his own life, and I told myself he didn't need to be saddled with his little sister forever. But eventually he began to see the truth. He started telling me I deserved better, that I should get out. When I finally made the decision, he was with me every step of the way."

Her voice wobbled toward the end. And Cooper was there, his arms around her, lending her warmth and support.

"I'm sorry, Nell," he said against her hair.

"I felt like I'd lost the last support I had in the world when he died," she said.

"But you kept going. I don't know if you really were as weak as you thought back then. More likely just shell-shocked. But it doesn't matter, because you're sure as hell not weak now. You got away, you built a life, you did everything you had to do."

And even as she savored it, relaxed into his embrace, she felt the difference; Cooper lent his support, but he knew she didn't need to be carried. He knew she wasn't what Jeremy had said she was.

He believed her. He believed *in* her.

And with that realization she felt the first spark of real hope about the situation that had seemed so devoid of it. She lifted her head, looked up at him. And then, unable to resist, she kissed him.

It was warm and comforting at first, but quickly flared into something more, something closer to the fiery heat they'd kindled in his bed. And when at last he pulled back, she wasn't sure if the tiny sound of protest she heard came from her or him.

"Careful," he said, his voice a little thick. "We'll end up back in bed."

"Promise?" she said, a little startled at her own shame-lessness. But there it was; for the first time in her adult life, she knew what it was to fully, truly, want a man. And she wanted this one. Again and again.

Cooper didn't wait for a second invitation. He picked her up and they were back in the master stateroom practically before she realized he was doing it. He began to undress her, and she sensed his tension building as he tried to go slow. She stilled his hands, and his gaze shot to her face. She could see he was wondering if she was changing her mind.

Changing her mind. Such a simple thing, yet a thing she hadn't been allowed for so long. Yet she knew down to her bones that even now, this man would stop if she asked him to.

The knowledge only served to flood her with even more heat, need and desperate want. She reached out to tug his shirt free of his waistband, eager to slide her hands over him again. Before, he'd done most of the exploring; now, she thought with a fervor that thrilled her even as it surprised her, it was her turn.

And when, clothes shed, they went down to the bed, still tossed from their first coming together, she began that journey. She worked her way over every inch of him, questing, learning, savoring every responsive twitch of muscle, every gasping breath when she stroked him here, kissed him there. As he had done to her, she learned him and she remembered.

She had thought that maybe her imagination had colored those hours, or that maybe they'd only been so incredible in comparison to the casual coldness she'd been used to. But now she knew better. This was more than just warmth in place of chill, ask in place of assuming, or want in place of coercion. This was fire, fierce and demanding and all-consuming.

When he rolled onto his back and pulled her over him, she realized he was giving her the lead. Or perhaps following her lead, letting her take the next step in her exploration. She nearly faltered, but then he reached up and cupped her breasts, catching and teasing her nipples between his fingers, and she cried out as her body clenched hard and low and deep.

And then she had to have him inside her again, had to have him ease that emptiness that had never been truly gone until the first time he'd slid into her body. She straddled him hastily, urgency in her every move. He gasped when she reached for him, fingers curling around his rigid length. She wanted to prolong it, to caress him, drive him mad with the kind of need she was feeling, but her own craving was too strong, too vital, to be postponed.

And when she took him home at last, she felt the triple shock of the sweet invasion, the convulsive tightening of his fingers on her hips as he arched to fill her, and the sweetest, hottest thing of all, the sound of her name breaking huskily from his lips, telling her one more time that she wasn't alone.

The soft whimper woke him. Nell lay with her back to him, curled up in a self-protective posture that got to him almost as much as the tiny sound she made did.

Nightmares.

He wasn't surprised. In fact, he'd have been surprised if she didn't have them.

He rolled over and tucked his body around her, gently, wishing he could protect her as easily as he could warm her. But they'd talked the better part of two days now, and she was still insistent Jeremy Brown couldn't be taken down. He realized she was speaking from years of dealing with him, years of intimidation and mental abuse, but he couldn't deny the man was a very powerful target. Nell was convinced going against him would be like going up against the Mafia with a slingshot.

And maybe she was right, he thought. Maybe they needed a new approach, a new idea. Maybe the traditional way of taking down a killer just wasn't right in this case. Not when they couldn't even prove he was a killer, not with the way he'd manipulated things into his favor, convincing people the only witness against him was unstable and untrustworthy long before it became an issue.

She stirred, whimpering again, and this time he couldn't stand it, he had to wake her out of whatever terror held her. He held her tighter, knowing she would likely awake with a start, then he whispered her name into the darkness.

On the third try she did indeed jerk awake, giving a little cry that was like a knife to his gut.

"Nell, Nell, it's all right. You're safe."

"Cooper?"

"Right here," he said, hugging her. And wishing that somehow he could make that always true.

Always?

The word echoed in his head, jolting him as much as that tiny cry had. His mind, as it usually did, skittered away from the thought of always. But somehow this time he had a suspicion it wouldn't go away just because he wasn't going to think about it.

And he wasn't, he told himself. He couldn't. He had to make sure she *had* an always before doing any thinking about being there for it.

"I'm sorry I woke you," she said into the darkness.

"Don't be," he said, hugging her against him.

"Okay, I take it back. I'm not sorry."

She reached for him then, and that quickly the fire between them reignited and flared. He was a little startled; he'd thought after her nightmare she'd just want to be held, reassured.

"Nell?"

"Burn it away," she whispered, and kissed him.

He did his best to do just that.

And much later, when dawn was approaching and they were sated for the moment—with anybody else Cooper would have been sated for days—they lay quiet, and he brought up the idea that had crystallized in his mind in the dark hours.

"What would you like to happen to him?"

She went still, as if she resented the intrusion of the man into the little, temporary paradise they had here. Truth be told, so did he, but that didn't change the necessity of dealing with the bastard.

Finally, with a sigh, she answered. "I'd like him to go down in flames. I'd like the world to know he didn't kill Tris in a heroic effort to save me, but that he's a stone-cold killer. I'd like him humiliated and publicly broken. Crass of me, isn't it?"

"No."

"Believe me, I know I'm not going to get that. He's just too strong, too powerful." She sighed. "But I'm tired of living every day in fear he'll find me."

"Then the real question is," he said, getting to it at last, "what would you settle for?"

"What?"

"Your 'Mafia and a slingshot' analogy," he said. "They couldn't get Al Capone for gangstering, so they took him down for tax evasion."

Her brow furrowed; he could see it now in the faint light coming in the porthole. "I get your point, but I don't understand how it relates to Jeremy."

"Sometimes all you have to use are the weapons you already have."

"Profound, I'm sure," she said, "but I still don't get it. What weapons do we have?"

He loved that she felt safe enough to throw a quip at him. But that was not where his head needed to be right now.

"What we have," he began, then paused before quashing his doubts and plunging on.

"What we have is you."

Chapter 28

She couldn't believe this was happening. Couldn't believe she was here, pacing like an animal in a cage.

And the hotel room, elegant though it was, was still a cage.

Vulnerable.

Trapped.

She felt like one of those goats they staked out in the jungle to lure in the lion. And the lion was close, she could almost feel him. She wanted to run, to get away, but Cooper was between her and the door. She'd told him she was tired of running, but she'd never expected to end up here, like this.

She crossed to the window, looked out. Seattle was a beautiful city, but a city still. She much preferred the quiet peace she'd found across the sound, in the more rural places.

When the knock came on the door she spun around, her heart hammering in her throat. But Cooper gave her no time to think about it, he just walked to the door and pulled it open.

And welcomed Jeremy Brown into the room as if he'd been a long-lost friend.

"Sorry about that," Cooper said, gesturing at Jeremy's swollen lip. "But I was pretty pissed."

Jeremy had only glanced at her, as if once he'd ascertained

she was indeed here she was worth no further scrutiny. But it was long enough for her to see the all-too-familiar rage banked there in his eyes, and she knew just how furious he was at her.

"She can have that effect," Jeremy said, in that convivial, man-to-man voice she'd heard him use on particularly difficult donors. He was wearing the same black coat over a different suit and tie; even now Jeremy was perfectly turned out. Although he was shifting his shoulders to settle the overcoat, as if it didn't fit quite right despite its obvious cost.

"You didn't have to lie to me," Cooper said.

"I apologize for that," Jeremy said, with every appearance of gracious sincerity. "I simply didn't want there to be any chance she might run again. If she doubted you, she might. Therefore you had to believe it yourself."

Cooper shrugged. "Yeah, I get it. Besides, the guy who's paying the bills calls the shots, right?"

"Speaking of that, the bonus has already been deposited in your account by transfer," Jeremy said. "And as we agreed, no charges will be filed after our…misunderstanding."

"Thanks."

"You drive a hard bargain, Mr. Grant," Jeremy said. "I admire that."

Cooper looked so flattered Nell felt a flutter of unease.

"I earned it," he said, jerking a thumb toward her without even looking at her. "She's a bit of a pain."

He hit the perfect note of wry impatience. So perfect that that flutter of unease grew into a full-fledged nervousness in her stomach.

"Oh, that I know too well," Jeremy said. "That's why I didn't argue much about that bonus."

"I did a little checking on you," Cooper said. "If I'd realized who I was dealing with before, I would never have made that stupid move, taking off with her like that."

"I'm sure you wouldn't have. But I couldn't have you telling her it was me who was looking for her. I counted on you not doing that kind of in-depth research."

For an instant Cooper went very still. "Oh?"

"Why do you think I picked you? I was told you were very, very good when motivated, but you tended to be a bit lackadaisical about the details. Which was exactly what I needed."

"I see."

"Oh, don't take it as a negative," Jeremy said heartily. "I'm sure there's a large market for that kind of investigation. The no-questions-asked kind."

Cooper smiled. The chilliness of it seemed obvious to Nell. But she had the odd sense the chill was directed inwardly.

"Maybe I've found a niche," Cooper said, his carefree tone at odds with that smile.

"Exactly!" Jeremy's voice was full of man-to-man good cheer. "And as I promised, I can do wonders for you. I know lots of people, wealthy people, who could use services like yours."

Nell stared at them. They sounded like two men who had reached common ground. They sounded like two men who had much in common. And she knew it was true; Jeremy could make Cooper a very busy—and very rich—man.

The nervousness in her stomach exploded into outright fear as Jeremy shifted his shoulders again, again adjusting the coat.

"And obviously you carried this off perfectly, getting her here without incident," Jeremy was saying. "She believed you?"

"Just like we planned. She thought this was all part of getting back at you."

Jeremy snorted inelegantly. "She would. As you said you've discovered, she's a fool."

He'd said that? That was a bit much, wasn't it? Nell felt herself go cold. Had this indeed all been a ruse to get her here?

To turn her over to Jeremy? Had Cooper never really stopped working for him?

But then why would he have helped her get away? Unless it was to get her to trust him. But why did he need her to trust him? He could have stopped her that day at the cottage and simply handed her over.

Her thoughts were like a dog chasing its tail, around and around and accomplishing nothing. And really, all her doubts did nothing, except make the bottom line clearer—if she had to believe Cooper had lied to her, that everything that had happened between them was a lie, then she might as well hand herself back to Jeremy, because he was obviously right and she was, literally, too stupid to live.

"—going to do with her?"

She snapped back to the present, telling herself she'd better pay attention. Cooper was either for real or he was a fraud, and she couldn't change either. She had to deal with what she'd gotten herself into. And deal with it herself.

Cooper's question had been asked with every appearance of only the mildest of curiosity.

"That's none of your concern," Jeremy said.

Cooper shrugged. "I was just thinking, you ought to let her jabber. What she says is crazy enough to put anybody who listens to her on your side."

Nell's stomach knotted. He sounded so…convincing. They'd talked about what the goal was, but not how he was going to go about it. But the only goal she could see nearing was her being back in Jeremy's hands.

Even as she thought it, Jeremy started across the room to her. This, she thought, was going to be the hardest part. Pretending she was beaten, when inside she was seething, when she wanted to strangle him with her bare hands.

Cooper's cell rang, and he excused himself and moved away slightly, turning his back on her as if he had no further interest in her.

"Come along, Tanya."

It stung bitterly to hear that name again, from him. And in that moment Nell's fear swamped her, and she was utterly certain Cooper had betrayed her, was truly going to let Jeremy drag her out of here without a second glance. She tried to fight it, then realized it changed nothing about what she had to do now. And there were other factors involved now. Surely even if Cooper cared nothing about her, he wouldn't go to those lengths if he—

Jeremy grabbed her arm. She jerked back as if burned.

"You think I'm just going to go with you quietly?"

"Of course you are."

He said it in the tone of a man certain he was being completely reasonable.

"After you murdered my brother?"

Jeremy shook his head as if saddened by her crazy words. "It was an accident, Tanya. The police know that. The media know that. You'd better accept it, or you're going to end up locked away and sedated somewhere."

As threats went, that was one of his better ones. It terrified her. For an instant she felt as if she were wobbling on some precipice, a hairsbreadth away from falling. And then, deep down, a spark flickered, then caught. Anger. She seized upon it. She was not doing this again. She would *not* let him win. Even if she was on her own.

"I'd rather be dead," she said flatly.

"Then don't do anything to put yourself in that situation, dear."

She went on as if he hadn't spoken. "Just like I'd rather be dead than spend one more second in your filthy, odious company."

His grip on her arm tightened. She dug in.

"You're scum, Jeremy. A manipulative parasite who uses a veneer of charm to feed off others."

"I can see you've learned some very bad habits, darling."

His tone was emotionless, but she'd seen the flicker in his eyes. She'd never dared confront him like that before. She couldn't tell if he was merely surprised, or if that shift in his eyes had been the start of anger. The latter, she hoped. She wanted him angry. She wanted him enraged.

"What I've learned is that there is no reason in the world to put up with someone like you," she said, letting every ounce of what she was feeling into her voice; if nothing else, he would hear the truth from her.

"My patience is getting short," he warned.

"That fits with all your other…shortcomings."

Jeremy's hand came off her arm and swung back, and she thought he might slap her. He'd never actually struck her before, but she didn't know if it was because it wasn't his sort of abuse, or because he'd had her so cowed it wasn't necessary. But the movement gave her the opportunity she needed; she was, for a moment, out of his grasp. She stepped back.

"Shut up."

He snapped out the order, clearly with every expectation of being obeyed. He took the step that put him back in her face, settling the coat on his shoulders yet again. Out of the corner of her eye, she saw Cooper move. He was closer to Jeremy now, his phone still in his hand, looking as if he were so focused on his call that he wasn't seeing or hearing a thing that was going on. Jeremy glanced at him, then refocused his gaze on her.

"I can see I've got my work cut out for me," he said, his tone grim.

"You've never worked an honest day in your life. You feed off the work of others. You're a leech—"

"Shut up," he said again.

"No."

Jeremy reached for her. She drew back. "Don't touch me. You're vile and repugnant, and you make my skin crawl."

There was no doubt about what flashed in his eyes then. She'd done it. Now to stoke it.

"Why don't you just kill me?" she said, pouring all her

disgust and loathing into her voice. "That's what you wanted to do that night."

"And it is to my eternal regret that I didn't."

Her breath caught. Was that enough? She wasn't sure, so she kept on. "But Tris stopped you."

"And now he's not here to save you, is he?" Jeremy sneered. "Be thankful. That's the only reason you're still alive now. Without him to protect you, you have nowhere to turn."

"I have myself," she said.

Jeremy laughed, a harsh, nasty sound. "Do you really think you can stand up to me? *Me?* The only reason you didn't die that night was that your stupid brother got in the way."

"That's how you did it, isn't it?"

Cooper's voice came from behind him. It seemed to take a moment for Jeremy to realize, through his fury, that Cooper's question was directed at him, that his phone call—or his pretense at a call—was over.

"What?"

"That's how you beat the lie detector. It really *was* an accident that night; you'd meant to kill *her,* not her brother. So you were able to say so honestly. Clever."

Cooper was speaking with every evidence of admiration, and after her insults, Nell was sure it was balm, proof that all was still right with his carefully constructed world.

"Yes, it was. I knew I could beat it. That's why I volunteered for it. Asked them to do it, so they could devote their time instead to finding my poor, distraught wife."

"Must have been a shock, her brother getting in the way like that."

"He always was a nuisance. I wasn't really sorry I hit him instead."

Instead. Wasn't that tantamount to an admission he'd intended to kill her all along?

"And there you have it," Cooper said cheerfully. And when he finally looked at Nell, he winked. Warmth and relief flooded her. "Nice job, blue eyes," he said.

Jeremy blinked. "What?"

"We're done here," Cooper said.

"What the hell are you talking about?"

"I'm talking about your admission that you intended to kill your wife, but that her brother got in the way. And your threat to kill her just now."

Jeremy nearly gaped at him. Nell wanted to laugh out loud, but she was too shaky to find the breath. She knew this didn't change the fact that Jeremy would somehow wiggle out of this if they tried to make him truly pay the price for what he'd done, but maybe, just maybe...

"You set me up," Jeremy said, outrage and disbelief ringing in his voice.

"Yep. And your stupid, unstable, pain of a soon-to-be-ex-wife played you like a flatheaded halibut."

He said it with such enjoyment Nell did laugh then. She'd been a fool all right. A fool to doubt him.

Her laugh sent Jeremy into pure fury.

"Nobody will believe you for an instant. Especially not the police. Some two-bit private eye and a crazy woman?"

"Yeah, you made sure everybody thought that, didn't you?" Cooper said.

He was still smiling, looking on the verge of laughing himself, and nothing could have been better calculated to send Jeremy over the edge. He was obviously, Nell thought, very sure they'd gotten enough. She only hoped he was right.

"You've made a very stupid decision, Grant. I'm a powerful man, with connections to the best lawyers in the country. And I *own* her."

"You have one choice," Cooper said, ignoring the declaration. "You stay out of her life. You don't fight the divorce, you don't say another word against or even about her."

"You're insane."

Cooper went on as if he'd never spoken. "You also retire any plans you ever had about public office. You're exactly what we've already got too much of in this country."

"Who the hell do you think you are?" Jeremy seemed, oddly, more amused than angry now. And that made Nell nervous.

"I tried to get Nell to shake you down for enough money so she didn't have to worry," Cooper said, "but she seems to find even your cash repulsive. So you can retire, and go live happily on some island somewhere."

"Retire? I'm not going to retire."

"Yes," Cooper said flatly, "you are."

"No," Jeremy said, "I'm not."

And Nell realized abruptly what had been behind the constant adjusting of the coat. It had been off balance. Weighted down on one side.

By the lethal-looking black handgun that had been in his pocket, but was now in his hand.

And aimed right at her.

Chapter 29

"I was afraid it might come to this," Jeremy said, with a display of regret so practiced that anyone who hadn't seen the other side of him would believe it was genuine.

But she had seen it, and too often. Not so long ago, she wouldn't have cared if Jeremy shot her dead. In fact, she would have welcomed it.

Nell was vaguely aware of Cooper making a gesture, throwing up a hand as if to say *halt,* but it wasn't aimed toward Jeremy. All she could really see was the gun the man she'd once trusted to keep her safe held. Surely it wasn't the same one? They would have kept that, wouldn't they? Not given it back to him?

She gave herself a mental shake; of course they would have. He'd convinced everyone it had been an accident, after all, and Jeremy was Jeremy, and could charm anything out of anyone.

"Put the gun down," Cooper said. His entire demeanor had shifted, all insouciance gone, nothing but deadly seriousness echoing in his voice.

"You're a fool, Grant," Jeremy said, never taking his eyes off her. Or the gun. "I could have made you rich."

"If you think you're just going to walk out of here, you're

the fool," Cooper said, taking a step forward at the same time. As if he, like Tris, was going to put himself between her and a bullet.

Jeremy was so focused on her he didn't seem to notice, but Nell did. It sent a frisson of fear racing up her spine. The scenario was so similar: her, a man on her side and Jeremy with a gun. Tris had ended up dead. She couldn't take that happening again. Especially not Cooper. Especially not this man she had, foolishly or not, gone and fallen in love with. The admission, made for the first time even to herself, wasn't even a shock. Perhaps shock couldn't find its way through the fear.

No. It wasn't going to happen again. She couldn't carry that, too. It would kill her. And if that was true, then she might as well make it a quick, clean death, not a lifetime of even more guilt and agony. She had to do something, and something that would assure that if someone again ended up dead at Jeremy's hands, it would be her.

"What was your plan, Jeremy?" she asked. "If you'd killed me? Hard to claim mistaken identity when it's your wife."

"I don't see why not," Jeremy said, as if she'd commented on the weather. "It was dark, I was frightened for you, I saw movement in the house where there shouldn't be… Of course, I would have had to kill your brother anyway. That way only my side of the story would be told. They would have believed me."

He'd clearly thought it through, which chilled her even more. Especially because she knew he was probably right, they would have believed him.

"So why didn't you just tell them I shot him?" she asked. "You could have said we struggled, explained the forensics. They would have believed you. People always do."

"Yes they do, don't they?" Jeremy said, his good cheer restored by once again having the upper hand. "But I had no intention of letting the police take you. Some pleasures I reserve for myself."

"You wanted to punish me yourself. For what? Daring to leave you?"

"You don't do anything without my permission," he said, as if it were the most reasonable assertion in the world.

"Go to hell, Jeremy."

He laughed, that smarmy, superior laugh she'd always hated. She nearly lunged at him then, and only the certain knowledge that she'd be dead before she got her hands on him—or that Cooper would be dead, after trying to stop her—kept her in place.

"You're a self-indulgent megalomaniac," Cooper said, taking another step.

"And you're a lazy bum who wastes what talents you have," Jeremy sneered. "And if you insist on interfering, you'll regret it."

"Like her brother did, you mean?" Cooper took the final step. Nell let out a sharp cry of protest as he put himself in the line of fire.

And then he did what she had nearly done—he lunged at Jeremy. He moved so quickly Nell gasped. And he didn't go for the weapon, instead he went in under Jeremy's raised arm. Plowed his shoulder into his chest. The gun went off, the bullet plowing into the ceiling. They both went down in a tangle. They rolled, Jeremy now on top. Then Cooper again. She'd lost sight of the gun, realized it was sandwiched between them somewhere.

In the instant she heard a crashing sound from behind them, another gunshot cracked, and she heard Cooper grunt. Her mind screamed *No!* even as someone else yelled from the doorway.

She grabbed the nearest thing she could put her hands on. Slammed it down as hard as she could into the side of Jeremy's head. He slumped, groaning. She dropped the silver hotel ice bucket from numbed fingers.

For an instant she knew she would never forget, neither

man moved. Terror filled her as for that instant, it seemed her worst nightmare had come to life once more.

And then Cooper moved. Shoved the still-dazed Jeremy off of him and sat up.

Shaking violently, Nell sank to her knees. She was barely aware of the other man who'd burst into the room, then come to a halt beside the three of them. Cooper scrambled the two feet between them and threw his arms around her. She hugged him back, fiercely.

After a moment, Cooper looked up at the newcomer, one of the men from the photograph on the wall of *The Peacemaker*. He was kneeling beside Jeremy and, thankfully, almost miraculously to Nell, handcuffing him.

"Hey, Dave," Cooper said when the man was done and turned to look at them.

"You cut that a little close, don't you think?" Dave said.

"Played the odds," Cooper said. "After stacking them a bit in my favor." He patted his oddly thickened chest. "I figured he used a gun once…anyway, thanks for the vest. And for being next door."

"You're lucky he didn't blow your head off."

Nell shuddered, while Cooper only shrugged. "That's why I got in close, fast."

Dave shook his head. "God, you remind me of your father."

Cooper went still. Nell squeezed him as he looked up at the man who had once been his father's partner.

"Thank you," Cooper said at last.

"Might not have been a compliment," Dave said, although his tone belied the words. "You took a hell of a chance."

"Nah," Cooper said, hugging her again. "I had backup handy."

The man smiled. "That you did." He looked at Nell and smiled. "And the video came through perfectly. Even he—" he thumbed a gesture at the now-reviving Jeremy "—isn't going to be able to grease his way out of this one."

Nell fingered the small flower pin fastened to the collar of her jacket. She knew such things as the little wireless camera existed, but she'd never expected to be wearing one.

But then, she'd never expected a lot of things that had happened in the last couple of weeks.

Including falling in love.

Especially falling in love.

Even by evening, Cooper was surprised his pulse rate had returned to normal. He'd thought it might stay permanently elevated. It had leaped into overdrive when Brown had pulled that gun on Nell, and it had been all he could do not to jump the guy right then. Only the knowledge that she could too easily be the one who got shot had kept him in control.

He'd wanted to do this alone, never would have risked Nell, but she'd been adamant. And he'd wondered for an instant, when she'd insisted on not wearing a bulletproof vest because it would give them away, if she was feeling suicidal.

"Never less," she'd told him, and something in her eyes as she had looked up at him had sent a shock wave through him. A tumult of emotions, fear, admiration, desire, need and, he was afraid, love, all tangled up and tagged with a label that said *forever,* which scared him even more. But there it was, and he'd known that when they got through this, he was going to have to face it.

And now it was here, and he was so damned glad she was okay that it didn't seem scary any longer, just inevitable.

She seemed to have relaxed the moment they stepped back aboard *The Peacemaker,* which pleased him. They were tied up in a guest slip connected to the condo building Dave lived in. His father's old partner had come through on all fronts, proving the truth of what Cooper had told her. The one thing he could bring to this that somebody else couldn't always get. As the son of a cop killed in the line, he could always get a hearing, even for what appeared to be an outlandish story.

"Cooper? Are you all right?"

He grimaced, didn't look at her as he went about the business of securing *The Peacemaker* for the night. "As all right as a guy can be who finds out he got picked for a job because he has a rep for being lazy."

"You're not lazy. Far from it."

"Careless, then."

"Casual, maybe," she said.

She was trying so hard to make him feel better it warmed him. "I let myself slide through," he said flatly. "I promised my mother I'd never become a cop, and then I used that as an excuse to not really become anything else."

"But you are," she insisted. "Look what you just did."

"You did it," Cooper said. "I just called in backup, and I could only do that because of my father. Who would," he finished with grim certainty, "be ashamed of me."

"I don't believe that for one second," Nell said. "But even if it were true, Dave is right. Your reputation is stellar now. You're going to have all the business you want after this, with your name all over the news."

He couldn't deny her point, since it was already happening. He'd always relied on word of mouth, and he'd gotten a ton of it in one day, with more, he was sure, to follow as the story spread wider. He hadn't really thought about that aspect of it, and wasn't proud that his first thought had been, *Whoa, not sure I want this!*

"Thank you for being a buffer for me, handling all the reporters and nosy types."

"No problem."

"Thank you for saving my life. Again."

"Back at you," he said. "That was a heck of a dent you put in ol' Jeremy's head with that bucket."

"Thank you for…believing me."

He stopped fastening down the last porthole window in preparation for the storm predicted to pass through tonight. Turned to look at her, remembered the expressions he'd seen flitting across her face as he played his part to Jeremy in that hotel room.

"You had your doubts there at the end, didn't you?"

"For a moment," she admitted, lowering her eyes.

"But you went ahead anyway."

She lifted her gaze back to his face. She drew in a breath, as if she were having to steady herself to speak. When she did, he understood why.

"Because if I had to believe you would betray me, I would rather have been dead anyway."

His own breath caught in his throat. He pulled her into his arms. "Never. Not you. Not ever."

"I know."

It was much later, when the rain began to fall and they were warm and sated and spooned together in the master berth, that Cooper, comfortably, wonderfully tired, finally spoke of the days ahead.

"It's going to be nasty," he said. "He won't go down without a fight, even with all we've got on him."

"I know."

"Dave is already digging. He said this would be the perfect big case to retire on, so he's going to be all damn-the-torpedoes on it. We'll bury him in the end."

"Yes." She said it with a quiet confidence that said volumes.

"You faced them down, Nell. All your demons. They're gone."

"Not all, but most. What about yours?"

He quashed the urge to make light of that. "My biggest one is myself. I'm working on it."

"I know. And you'll succeed."

"Such faith."

"Yes."

Again that quiet confidence. In him. "Nell?"

"What?"

"I…" He chickened out. "Shall we head back in the morning,

after the storm? I know you talked to Roger, but he'd probably like to see for himself that you're okay."

She moved, snuggling herself into the curve of his body, and setting off a chain reaction that would have him hot and wanting her all over again in a matter of moments.

"Thank you. I'd like that. And you need to get your bike, too."

"Mmm-hmm." God, she was so incredibly sexy, all tousled and warm and soft against him.

"And after that…"

Her voice trailed off, and he reined in his eager body. "You have things to deal with there, I know. But then…whenever you're ready…"

She went still as he fumbled for the words. "Whenever I'm ready, what?"

"We should point *The Peacemaker* south. A nice long sail, so you can get your head together while we get you back to L.A. So you can…properly say goodbye to Tristan."

In the darkness he heard her breath catch. "I…don't even know where he is."

"He's next to your mom."

She jolted up on one elbow. "What?"

"The name Alex Ayala ring a bell?"

"Tris's best friend."

"He saw to it." At her questioning look he added, "I made a couple of calls while Dave was sorting things out. Didn't take long."

"You really are good," she said.

"Say that again in about ten minutes," he whispered against her ear, slipping one hand down to cup her breast.

"I usually do," she teased right back.

There was indeed something different about her now, a lightness, a freedom she expressed with a fierce eagerness that took his breath away. And before it was over he was glad of the pounding rain, because it would muffle the shout of her name that he didn't even try to stop.

And much later, when she quietly thanked him yet again, he found the words and the nerve. And when she shyly returned his unpracticed declaration, the knot of tangled emotions slipped apart easily and seemed to wrap around them both, binding them inextricably in a way that was, to his surprise, not confining but freeing.

Amazing what a simple "I love you, too" could accomplish, he thought.

In this case, it changed his life. And if a land-bound office or house—*or home,* he corrected—was in his future, well, it was suddenly a lot more appealing.

But for now, he had Nell and *The Peacemaker* and the sea was calling.

Epilogue

This third time would be her last visit to Tris's grave, at least for now. That flock of vultures some called the media had made it too difficult, for her, for the small cemetery and for Cooper, who tried to keep them at bay with a constant litany of "She has no comment." So today she'd come in the predawn hour. And finding the place as she'd hoped, empty, Cooper had retreated to give her peace and privacy, this time to say goodbye.

She didn't think she would ever get used to his intuitiveness, his concern for her thoughts and her feelings. She'd spent too long with a man who cared nothing for either to take his perceptiveness for granted. And whenever she wavered, felt weak, he reminded her that no weak woman could have done what she did, gone through what she did, and come out whole.

She hadn't told him, yet, that he was the only reason she had gotten through the last weeks.

The leisurely sail down from Seattle had been a glorious respite. There were so many things hovering, including what on earth she was going to do with herself when this was over. Cooper just held her and said she could figure that out later, and that as long as he was in the picture, he didn't care what she did. Or if she did anything. And then he'd made such sweet love to her that the future seemed almost impossibly bright.

He had kept her insulated from the reality she knew she'd have to deal with later, keeping her apprised himself, but only if she asked. Cooper had shown her one picture that came close to encapsulating her wish. Jeremy, in handcuffs, being marched past a crowd of reporters, looking furious and… worried. She'd never seen him look like that, and it gave her a jab of satisfaction.

It had been when they'd gotten close, after a brief stop in Santa Barbara, that Cooper had warned her the story was still the top of the news, and that her whereabouts was near the top of every story.

She'd known the case would be high profile down here, where Jeremy had been headquartered, but she hadn't really realized how massive the interest would be. At least one news outlet had had somebody watching the cemetery where Tristan was buried next to their mother. Cooper had kept him occupied, trying to give her time and space to grieve as she'd never really had the chance to before.

But soon there were too many, and then the wheels of justice had caught her, and she'd spent hours upon hours with investigators. She found that Cooper had paved the way; he'd told them exactly why she'd run, that she hadn't trusted them not to do what was right instead of what they might feel pressured to do with someone like Jeremy. And he'd challenged them to prove her wrong, which they now seemed determined to do. Maybe they would have been from the beginning, but she had no way of knowing.

She reached out to brush a leaf from the simple headstone that bore her beloved brother's name. She'd thanked Alex for that, and for seeing that Tris was buried here, and she'd been thankful that he'd kept the questions to a minimum when he'd obviously been full of curiosity. Later, she thought, she'd tell him what she could.

She lay the simple bouquet of carnations—puffballs, Tris

had called them when they were kids—across his name. Then she turned to the headstone beside his to lay the second bouquet, this one her mother's favorite: lilies. Cooper had found the florist for her, who had managed both this late in the year.

She sat between the two graves. The beautiful shimmer of happiness ahead, with Cooper, was the only thing that kept her from wanting to join them. She was thoroughly alone now; the only blood family who had truly loved her lay here.

She noticed Cooper approaching, with another man just behind him. He looked to be older, maybe in his fifties, casually dressed. Another reporter? No, Cooper wouldn't let him get close. It must be another detective or D.A.'s investigator or someone like that.

Knowing she didn't have long, she reached out, put a hand on each headstone and summoned up their images in her mind. Her mother, before her illness, healthy, happy, with that glint of humor always in her eyes. Her brother, grinning, windblown and with that same glint, inherited as he'd inherited so much from their mother.

"I love you," she whispered, "and I always will. And I know you love me. I will miss you both every day of my life. But I'm going to be all right. I promise you that."

She simply sat there then, wishing for something she didn't know how to name, some sort of feeling or sign or presence, something she would no doubt laugh at herself for later. But here and now, in this place, she couldn't help hoping that—

"Nell?"

Cooper knelt beside her, reaching out a hand. She took it, and his strong fingers wrapped around hers, warming them in the early morning chill. The sun was clearing the hills to the east now, but it hadn't warmed the air yet.

"I don't mean to interrupt—" he began, but stopped when she shook her head.

"It's all right. I was starting to get silly."

He took her other hand. And something in the way he was looking at her told her she needed to pay real attention.

"What?"

"Do you love me?"

They'd established that rather thoroughly on the sail down here, she'd thought, but she answered anyway, simply.

"Yes."

"Remember that, if you start to get mad at me."

She drew back, puzzled. "Mad at you? What on earth for? You've done nothing but help and—"

This time she stopped at the shake of his head. "I did something," he began.

"Cooper?" she prompted when he stopped.

But he didn't go on. Instead, he tugged her to her feet. Then he turned her around, so she was facing the man standing six feet away. He looked familiar, but she didn't think it was from the round of sessions she'd been having with the police and prosecuting attorneys.

And then she noticed that his cheeks were wet, as if he'd been crying. As if he still was. He made no effort to wipe away tears, he simply stood there, staring at her.

With her own blue eyes.

Her breath caught.

"Hello, trout-hugger," he said, his voice tight.

"Daddy?" she whispered, feeling for an instant like the child who had uttered that appellation with such adoration.

She saw Cooper move, start to back away, to leave them alone. This man she had once been so angry with for lying to her, and now filled her with such love it nearly overwhelmed her. This man who had stood by her every step of the way. This man who had done so much to smooth a rough, difficult path for her. This man who had made her realize the truth about her long-held anger.

This man who had now, quietly, without a word, given her back the one last remaining thread of her own family.

He was watching her warily, obviously uncertain how she

would take this, if what he'd done would be welcome. As if she could ever be mad about the biggest declaration of love she'd ever seen in her life.

She met his gaze head-on.

"I love you," she said.

She saw him let out a long, relieved breath.

"I love you, too," he said.

"I know. More than ever, I know."

He smiled. She smiled back, putting everything she could of what she was feeling into it.

And then she accepted his gift.

She held her hand out to her father.

* * * * *